My Boy John that Went to Sea

My Boy John
that Went to Sea

By James Vance Marshall

Illustrations by Lydia Rosier

WILLIAM MORROW & COMPANY, INC.

New York 1967

Acknowledgments

Passages from *The Light of the Western Stars* Copyright 1914 by Harper & Bros., Copyright 1941 by Lina Elise Grey, are quoted by kind permission of the Zane Grey Estate, Inc., California.

The Map of Graham Land is reproduced from Admiralty charts 3205 and 3570 by permission of The Royal Geographical Society, London.

Text copyright © 1966 by Hodder and Stoughton Ltd.

Published in Great Britain in 1966.
Published in the United States in 1967.

Illustrations for the American edition copyright © 1967 by Lydia Rosier.

Printed in the United States of America.

Library of Congress Catalog Card Number 67-15153

Author's Note

Each summer about ten thousand men go south to Antarctica to hunt the whale. This is the story of a handful of these men, the crew of the S.S. *Petrel*. It is a story that is based on fact, and in telling it I have taken no liberties with the technicalities of whaling. The footsteps of the blue, the strain on the tow, and the slant of the *Petrel's* deck are real; only the characters owe anything to imagination.

J. V. M.

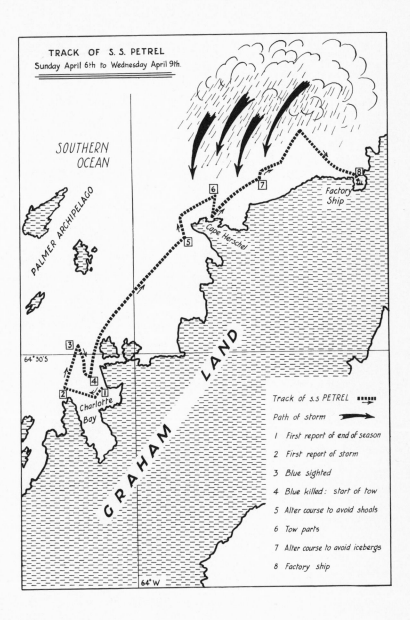

TRACK OF S.S. PETREL
Sunday April 6th to Wednesday April 9th.

SOUTHERN OCEAN

PALMER ARCHIPELAGO

Cape Herschel

Factory Ship

64° 30' S

Charlotte Bay

GRAHAM LAND

64° W

Track of s.s PETREL ▪▪▪▪▪▪
Path of storm ➤

1 First report of end of season
2 First report of storm
3 Blue sighted
4 Blue killed: start of tow
5 Alter course to avoid shoals
6 Tow parts
7 Alter course to avoid icebergs
8 Factory ship

Ho, sailor of the sea!
How's my boy, my boy?
My boy John
That went to sea?
What care I for the ship, sailor?
My boy's my boy to me.

Sidney Thompson Dobell

Prologue
Tuesday, January 7th

It was 5 A.M. and the fields of ice lay grey and silent under the stars as the whalecatcher S.S. *Petrel* stood out from the coast of Graham Land.

Most of the *Petrel's* crew were already on deck. Soon they would be searching for the blows of humpback, sperm and fin—for it was the first day of the whaling season—but for the moment all they were thinking about was their tea. They collected it from the galley: steaming mugs of rum-laced tea which they drank gratefully, stamping their feet on the deck and blowing away the steam to prevent it condensing to ice on their beards.

The deckie watched them. He barely came up to their shoulders, but in his oilskins, Wellingtons and heavy fur-flapped cap he felt very much a man. When he was sure that the rest of the crew had been given their tea, he too went to the door of the galley. He held out his mug, and when it had been filled he pushed it, as he had seen the others push theirs, alongside the bottle of rum.

It was old Johan, the cook, who was dispensing tea. Johan was fond of the deckie, but he was not at all sure that he ought to let him have rum; so he turned for advice to the mate. And the mate shook his head. He too was well disposed towards the boy and knew that a tot would do him no harm, but he *was* the skipper's son, and the skipper had made it plain that he wanted no favourites aboard. So the mate picked up the bottle of rum and locked it away in the spirit store. "Not for you, young 'un."

"Why not, Torstein?"

"Not till you're grown up."

The hurt was no less painful for being unintended. The boy didn't particularly want the rum; but he *did* want to be treated as one of the crew, to share everything with them, hardships and pleasures alike. His voice was wistful: "When will I be grown up?"

A little coterie of whalers, joining casually in the conversation as they returned their empties to the galley, made half-humorous, half-serious suggestions—"When you've heard the blue whales singing, then you'll be a real man o' the world"; or, "When you know what's t'other side of an iceblink." Only old Johan gave the boy an answer that he could understand: "Bein' grown up," he said, "ain't jest a matter of bein' tall and havin' big muscles. It means bein' sort of big inside."

The boy thought about this. He had to admit it made

sense; and yet it rankled that he was being treated differently to the others. He put down his mug. "If I can't have rum in it," he said, "I don't want any tea at all!"

He knew he was being silly. He regretted the words the moment they were out of his mouth, but he was too proud to take them back. He walked aft and sat by the truck of the mizzen.

* * *

It was only a very little thing—their not allowing him rum the same as the rest of the crew—and if, as the season progressed, the boy had been happy, the incident would have been quickly forgotten. But he was not happy. For he found that life in a whalecatcher was very different to what he had dreamed of. Back home there had been an obvious bond of affection between himself and the crew. He had stayed in their homes, played with their children, and listened enthralled to their fo'castle yarns of the far south; he had been like one of their family. But aboard *Petrel* the bond of comradeship seemed to have been replaced by the fetter of discipline. And the boy didn't like it. Why, he asked himself with increasing chagrin as the weeks passed, did the crew have to treat him not as one of themselves but as a child? He was doing a man's work; he was almost as tall as Johan. Couldn't they *see* he was growing up?

Apparently they couldn't. And gradually, as summer gave way to autumn, the events of that first morning came to assume in the boy's mind a quite disproportionate significance; and by the time the season was nearing its end he had carved ninety-one notches in the foot of the mizzen: one for each of the mornings that he had sat there alone, watching the rest of the crew as they laughed and joked together over their mugs of rum-laced tea.

1.

Sunday, April 6th

It was one of those autumn days near the end of the whaling season when from the flame of dawn to the euthanasia of the long Antarctic twilight everything had gone well. The weather had been dreamlike; in the fourteen hours of daylight they had killed seven whales (only one more and the longed-for bonus would be theirs), and as the boy watched the great gold disc of the sun sink into the ice he was smiling.

He was slight, fair-haired and fourteen, with big brown eyes that dwarfed the rest of his face and a mouth as obstinate as his father's. From the raptness of his expression he might have been lost in the beauty of the sunset—the apple-green sky and the iridescent shafts of light reflected and refracted by the ice into every colour of the spectrum—but in fact the beauty of the evening passed him by. For he was dreaming, dreaming of a world that was far removed from the lonely wastes of Antarctica.

He was, in his dreams, in a concert hall, seated at a piano. He had just played his favourite Chopin mazurka, and the audience were on their feet, wild with applause. He could see the white and clap of their hands, he could hear the excitement of their shouts—"Encore! Encore!" —and he was happy, happier than he had been for months on the storm-lashed deck of the *Petrel*.

It was an unexpected dream perhaps for a boy whose forebears had been whalers for generations. But his mother—who was English by birth and had adopted Norwegian nationality only after her marriage—had spent several years studying music at the Sorbonne. She had adored the piano, which she played with no little skill, and she had passed her love of music on to her son.

She had started to teach him as soon as his hands were able to span a chord. By the time he was five he could play not only nursery rhymes like *"Ride, ride ranke"* and *"Bao, bao lille lam,"* but also one or two simple Mozart sonatas; and by the time he was six his repertoire had widened to include the Bach inventions, a few pieces of early Scarlatti and Grieg's "Watchman's Song," "Arietta" and "Waltz." It would be an exaggeration to describe the boy as a genius or even a prodigy. But he had a very definite flair. And this flair his mother encouraged, recognizing in his embryo love of music a counterattraction to the call of the Antarctic which her instinct told her would one day claim her son as it had already claimed her husband. But the dreams that they dreamed together were never fulfilled. For suddenly, a few days after John's seventh birthday, his mother died—died in the maternity wing of an Oslo hospital together with the sister he was never to see.

After her death the boy didn't give up the piano altogether. But from that day onward, whenever his fingers moved over the keys, he was never quite sure if he was playing for love of music or for love of the mother whom he missed more deeply than he ever cared to admit.

The clapping of hands grew louder and the shouting harsher. John Larsen opened his eyes and saw not the audience of his dreams but his father, gesticulating angrily. He jumped to his feet and scrambled onto the bridge.

"Dreaming again, lad!" His father's voice had a touch of exasperation.

"I'm afraid I was."

Svend Larsen walked to the rail. He was a thickset, powerful man, slow-moving, slow-thinking, and not much given to words. More than half of his forty-six years had been spent in the lonely waters of the south, and whaling was something he understood; but he didn't understand his son. For more than a decade he had been looking forward to the time when the boy would be old enough to come whaling with him and the two of them could sail the Antarctic together, lashed by the same storms, marvelling at the same iceblinks, sharing their moments of triumph and despair; and when John had come south for the first time as *Petrel's* deckie his cup of happiness had been full. But things hadn't worked out. His son hadn't taken to whaling. And Svend Larsen couldn't understand why. . . .

To start with, everything had seemed to go well. As they had worked their way south in *Cyclopean* (the factory ship which left Norway each autumn and returned the following summer with her tanks full of whale oil to the value of millions of dollars) the boy had been happy. He had been happy when they crossed the equator, and happy when they put ashore in the Falkland Islands, but as soon as they transferred from *Cyclopean* to *Petrel* things began to go wrong.

They boy's first shock had been the physical discomfort of life in a whalecatcher. He had been brought up mostly by his grandparents who, as is the way with grandparents the world over, had spoiled him, and he was unprepared for the cramped quarters and numbing cold of the sea lanes south of Cape Horn. He was unprepared, too, for the cruelty—the first time he saw a dying fin, cascading blood, dragged belly-up under the whale-catcher's bow he was violently sick, and the great creature's death agony (which he witnessed on an average two or three times a day) was something he never became inured to. His disenchantment with whaling would have been less acute if he had had a friend with whom he could talk things over. The obvious person for him to turn to was his father. But the moment they transferred ship, their relationship underwent a change: in *Cyclopean* his father had been his companion; in *Petrel* he was his commanding officer. It would be an oversimplification to say that as soon as the whaling season started Svend Larsen neglected his son; but he had a horror of nepotism, and he made it clear that he expected his boy to be treated as an ordinary deckie—neither better nor worse—and that *his* job as *Petrel's* skipper was to kill whales and not wet-nurse the least important member of his crew. And the boy (who was sensitive and reserved by nature) took his cue from his father. Anxious not to presume on their relationship, he kept his troubles to himself, bottling up his discontent until it matured into an unhappiness that was all the greater for being so carefully concealed. If he had been older, he might have enjoyed the companionship inherent in being one of a crew. But at fourteen he was the youngest aboard by nearly five years—in terms of maturity almost another generation. Also, and this was the real kernel of the boy's discontent, he never felt that he *was* one of the crew; he was only the deckie, a sort of supernumerary dogsbody who, it seemed, had by tradition to serve his apprenticeship before he was accepted as a whaler. A less sensitive boy might not have minded being treated differently to the others. But John Larsen was all too conscious of the fact that his food was always served to him last, that while the others were known by their Christian names he was always called "deckie," and that his morning tea was pushed across without the traditional tot of rum.

And so, as the weeks passed, the boy came to retire more and more into his shell, seeking refuge from the harsh realities of the present in the make-believe world of his dreams.

It was always his music he dreamed of—of the thunder of orchestras and the applause of audiences—and increasingly often as the season progressed among the audience of his dreams he saw the face of his mother, smiling the proud, gentle and approving smile that he had basked in in the days of his childhood. He had been basking in it again when he heard the shout from the bridge . . .

"Dreaming again, lad!"

"I'm afraid I was."

Svend Larsen walked to the rail. He didn't need to ask what his son was dreaming about. He knew. He stared at the sunset. The sky was green as apple mint now and the sun was sinking into a sea as gold as a field of corn, and it seemed to Larsen impossible that anyone could fail to be moved by so much beauty. He made a little gesture towards the disappearing disc of the sun. "Doesn't this mean anything to you?"

The boy didn't answer at once. It made him unhappy to know he was disappointing his father, and he did at times, as through a glass darkly, catch a glimpse of something almost sublime in the limitless expanse of sea and ice; but most of the while he felt more awe than love. "I'm sorry, Dad," he said at last, "but I can't say I *really* like it."

It was the answer Larsen had expected, but its finality depressed him. Sadness seeped into him, a sadness as all-pervading as the fog that drifts inshore with the autumn ice, grey and cheerless and chill. Maybe, he thought, I should never have brought the boy whaling; maybe the hopes I have cherished all these years have been selfish. "Tell me, John"—his voice was gentle—"what do you want most, more than anything else in the world?"

The boy had expected to be given a job or a message, not pitchforked suddenly into a heart-to-heart talk for which he was unprepared. He moistened his lips. "Don't really know."

"Let's have a straight answer, lad."

For a moment John Larsen's eyes met his father's, then they dropped. "I want," he said, "to study at the Academy."

"In Copenhagen?"*

"Yes."

"You'd need extra tuition first. Then there's the cost of living in a foreign capital for, say, five years—why, it would cost the better part of ten thousand dollars."

"Oh, I know it's impossible. But you *did* ask."

Svend Larsen's hands closed over the rail. He wanted something to hang on to, tightly, while he said a final good-by to the dreams of fourteen years. "It's not impossible at all," he said at last. "In fact, you can go to the Academy in the spring. I'll give you *Petrel's* bonus to pay your fees."

* State-sponsored education in Norway has no provision for making grants to students of music, who are obliged to study either privately or in the Academy at Stockholm or Copenhagen.   J.V.M.

The bonus Larsen was giving away was the desideratum of every Antarctic skipper. Each year the owners offered an award of $10,000—the value of a single blue— to the first whalecatcher to return two hundred whales to its factory ship. *Petrel* had already returned a hundred and ninety-nine (a score more than her nearest rival), and nothing, it seemed, could now prevent Larsen from claiming the award—an award which by tradition was split one-third to the skipper and two-thirds among the crew. . . .

The boy stared at his father, not daring to believe what he had heard. "You'll do what?"

"I'll give you the bonus. To pay your fees."

It was too wonderful to be true. Scenes that he had dreamed of for years came floating by out of the dying sun: the crowded concert halls, the hushed auditoriums, the cheers, the applause and the rave reviews, their outline given substance by the knowledge they now had a chance of coming true. He didn't know what to say; words were inadequate. "Oh, Dad!" was all he could whisper. "Thanks!" For a moment his happiness was absolute. Then came a sudden doubt. "But what about the crew? Don't you have to share the bonus with *them?*"

"It was the crew's idea," Larsen said, "that I give the money to you."

Again the boy could hardly believe his ears. For although none of the crew had ever been unkind, they had always seemed so aloof; they had kept him so very much in his place and had given no hint that they even knew of his dreams—let alone cared about them. He felt quite suddenly that things had been going on in *Petrel* that he hadn't begun to understand. He stood by his father, thinking, looking out at the darkening sea. "Dad!"

"Hmmm?"

"Whose idea was it, to give me the bonus?"

"I reckon the crew decided together, among themselves."

"When?"

"Two or three weeks ago. The night we got back from *Cyclopean.*"

The boy nodded. He remembered the occasion well. . . .

The weather had been bad that afternoon in late March when *Petrel* had come alongside the factory ship to refuel. Bunkering had taken four hours instead of the usual two, and when their tanks were full Larsen had not put back to sea but had sought shelter with the rest of the catchers in the lee of an ice wall. By sunset it was obvious that conditions were too bad for whaling, and the master of *Cyclopean* had invited aboard as many of the whalecatcher crews as could be spared from their ships. In *Petrel* they had drawn lots to decide who should go. Torstein, Johan, the deckie and the brothers Carl and Bengt Nielsen were lucky, and a little after 9 P.M. the five of them were hoist aboard *Cyclopean* in a supply basket.

The stability of the forty-thousand-ton factory ship made a welcome change to *Petrel's* continual pitch and roll. There were luxuries to buy from the store, old

friends to talk to, and by 10 P.M. a variety of parties were under way. After a while John Larsen found himself in the lower saloon, where the meat-meal-foreman was thumping away with more enthusiasm than skill on *Cyclopean's* only piano. It wasn't long before the boy was spotted.

"Ah, here's young Larsen. Make way for your betters, Dornoch!"

The foreman slid off his stool, and the boy, protesting, was pushed towards the piano.

He was nervous at first; uncertain, among other things, of what they expected him to play. He started with a couple of pop tunes, switched to the hits from a current musical, and then tried to get up—"Let someone else have a turn." But they persuaded him to go on. He thought at first they were simply being kind, but after a while the truth got home: they really *liked* listening to him. And so, as the haze of cigarette smoke thickened and spread and the saloon filled gradually to capacity, the boy played on and on. He played Gilbert and Sullivan and blues, rock-and-roll and New Orleans jazz, Christmas carols and songs by Björnson, and whenever he tried to stop they filled him up with Pepsi-Cola and shouted and stamped until he sat down again on his stool. By midnight his non-classical repertoire was exhausted, and he began to play Grieg's Piano Concerto. His audience were *sympathique* (glad to relax and be entertained; they saw in the slight fair-haired figure at the piano a reminder of their far-off families and homes), and the boy, sensing their mood, played as he had seldom played before. This to him was happiness: just to lose himself in the music, with thought of neither criticism nor applause. And it was more than a rendering of Grieg's Piano Concerto that he gave that night in the saloon; it was a Performance, technically flawless and interpreted with a freshness and enthusiasm that would have won the hearts of a far more critical audience than *Cyclopean's*. When the last note faded and died there was a moment of surprised silence, then wave after spontaneous wave of applause, long and loud, as in the happiest of his dreams.

No one was pleased, a few minutes later, to hear *Petrel's* foghorn blaring the signal to return.

The five didn't say much as they were swung across to the whalecatcher. John was too happy and the whalers too preoccupied—they couldn't get over the metamorphosis: how the child who served them with tea from *Petrel's* galley had blossomed out at the piano into a mature and dedicated artist. As soon as the boy was below and asleep they talked things over over a nightcap of cocoa. It was Bengt Nielsen who put into words what they had all been thinking: "Always knew he could play. But I never knew he could play like that!"

For a while they were silent, thinking, blowing the steam off their mugs; then the mate turned to Johan: "Has Svend got the lad down for the Academy?"

The old whaler shook his head. "He's thought about it. But ten thousand dollars takes a deal o' saving."

"Hmmm! Be handy if we could win the bonus!"

The idea didn't catch on at once, for seamen the world over are cautious and conservative by nature. But they slept on it, chewed it over, and canvassed it among the rest of the crew; and they eventually found, rather to their surprise, that they all felt the same: they were prepared to forego their share of the bonus to pay the boy's fees at the Academy.

Their generosity stemmed from the love that they felt for Svend and his son. Svend Larsen was one of the best-liked skippers in the Antarctic fleets. For years he had kept the same crew, welding them with love, patience and care into the likeness of a united family. As for the boy, ever since the death of his mother he had been unofficially adopted by *Petrel*'s crew, and the men had come to think of him almost as one of their flesh and blood. It is true that aboard *Petrel* they had kept their feelings under rein—for long-standing tradition demanded that a deckie should prove himself before he was accepted into the almost mystical fraternity of whalers—but their affection had been none the less deep for being concealed. They had been quick to see that the boy was none too happy

with life in a whalecatcher, and late one evening towards the end of March Torstein had a talk with his skipper.

Although Larsen was deeply touched by the crew's offer, his first impulse had been to turn it down. "The men," he argued, "have enough family commitments of their own without taking on mine." But Torstein had said simply, "You talk of family commitments. But surely the crew are all of one family too." And after a discussion that spanned the dog watches Larsen was persuaded to accept. It would, he told himself, be churlish to look a gift horse such as this in the mouth, and although he himself still longed for his son to stay whaling with him, it was only right that he should subjugate *his* dreams to the boy's. He had said nothing to his son at the time, not wanting to raise false hopes; but there could be no harm, he thought, in telling him now. . . .

They stood by the rail watching the colour drain slowly out of the sky. For a while the boy was too happy for words. Then came a sudden fear.

"Dad!"

"Hmmm?"

"We need one more whale for the bonus."

"Reckon we're sure to get it."

"But what if the weather breaks? Or they end the season?"

Larsen laid a hand on his son's shoulder. The words came easily, with no presentiment of fear and no premonition of disaster: "We'll get you one more whale," he said. "I promise."

As the light faded and the stars crept one by one into a cloudless sky, they talked of the Academy. Not for months had they felt so much at ease with one another, and not until the aurora had begun to flicker along the horizon and the frost to glint on hawsers and spars did they make their way below.

The sky grew darker, the stars brighter; by midnight the crew of the *Petrel* slept.

Most of them that night, worn out by fifteen hours of whaling, slept the sleep of the physically exhausted. But Larsen dreamed, and so did his son.

Svend Larsen dreamed that he was on *Petrel's* bridge; great seas were sluicing green the length of the deck, and his son was beside him, laughing, as together they hunted pod after pod of blue in a chase that went on and endlessly on till his son was a boy no longer. But the boy dreamed of another world: of the surge and thunder of music, of crowded concert halls, and the applause of audiences and orchestras. This was the gulf that divided them, that they loved one another but dreamed of a different rainbow's end.

And as they dreamed their dreams, up through the islands of the Palmer Archipelago came their two hundredth whale, the great bull blue which held the key to all that they hoped and prayed for.

The blue was restless, sensing a change in the weather long before the most delicate instruments of the meteorologists. Cobalt and grey in colour, a hundred feet in length and a hundred and fifteen tons in weight, he swam slowly north, now feeding on the drifting shoals of squid, now surfacing to blow at the stars of the Southern Fish. He too was dreaming: of the cows he had served off the Chilean shore, of the giant squid he had fought in the depths of the sea, of the storms his strength and experience had enabled him to ride.

And so, each wrapped up in his own little world, they dreamed away the Antarctic night, the man, the boy and the great bull whale.

But the Antarctic is no respecter of dreams.

2.

Monday, April 7th

It was the signal that touched off the trail to the powder keg. It arrived a little after 1 A.M.: CYCLOPEAN TO ALL CATCHERS. WHALING SEASON WILL TERMINATE* MIDNIGHT TUESDAY APRIL 8TH. ACKNOWLEDGE.

When he had read back and entered the signal the radio operator took it to the bridge. There were only the two of them awake—he and the helmsman—and together in the soft red glow of *Petrel's* bow lights they peered at the unwelcome message.

"Leaves us less than forty-eight hours!" The operator was indignant.

* The whaling season ends each autumn, not on a certain day that is known in advance, but after the catching of a certain number of whales. When the combined haul of the pelagic fleets nears this permissible total, a signal is sent by the International Whaling Board to every factory ship saying that the season will end at such and such a moment; after this moment no whales may be accepted for processing.

J.V.M.

"Should be enough—for one whale."

"Unless the weather breaks . . . You reckon we ought to call Svend?"

"Let him sleep. We can't whale in the dark."

They talked for a while of the iniquities of the Whaling Board in giving them so little notice of the season's end—usually whalecatchers were given three clear days, hardly ever less than two—then the radio operator went back to his cabin. But he didn't go there direct. He made a detour en route to look at the barometer. The barometer was reading exactly the same as it had read for days, 30.68, as steady as the proverbial rock. So there was no indication, the operator told himself, that the weather was going to change. But at the back of his mind were the seeds of anxiety. For the night had a breathlessness that he didn't like.

About half an hour later the helmsman, too, felt the need to look at the barometer. It still read 30.68. And so he, like the radio operator, told himself that he must be imagining things and returned to his job.

But a little after 2 A.M. their fears were confirmed.

Blood-red and haloed wickedly, the moon flared up like an oriflamme from out of the fields of ice, and the helmsman, as he stared at it, felt a stab of fear. For a haloed moon in Antarctica is an augury of storm.

As the moon climbed higher it increased in size and brilliance until the bright concentric circles of its halo seemed to be swallowing the sky. By 3 A.M Aquarius and the Southern Fish had been blotted out, and sea and ice were bathed in a dull red light, like the glow from a volcano seen through falling ash. Not in twenty years in the Antarctic had the helmsman seen a more evil moon, and *Petrel* was on a lee shore. He had no compunction now in reaching for the captain's voice pipe.

Svend Larsen surfaced reluctantly from the happiness of his dreams, unhooking the speaking tube by instinct while he was still only half awake. "Yes?"

"Carl here, skipper. Season ends midnight tomorrow."

"Hmmm!" The helmsman could picture him checking his watch. "Leaves us forty-five hours. Should be enough for a dozen whales, let alone one."

"But that's not all. The moon's got a nasty halo."

He was jerked wide-awake, like a man toppled straight from bed to an ice-cold bath. "Is the glass falling?"

"Not yet."

"Any gale warnings?"

"No."

"But you reckon we're in for a storm?"

"Real rogue, by the look o' it."

The helmsman's anxiety got through to Larsen, and he swung his legs over the side of the bunk and said he'd be up. He dressed carefully—string underwear, canvas overalls, lamb's-wool jacket and heavy fur-lined oilskins. He stuffed balaclava and gauntlets into his pocket, rubbed cream and Vaseline onto his face, and climbed on deck.

It was too still and too quiet. The concentric circles around the moon were expanding and contracting as though the night were panting for breath, and the

optimism that Larsen had basked in yesterday gave way
to a sudden pyramiding of doubts—what if the storm was
on them before they could make their kill? What then
of their bonus and the promise he had made to his son?
He ought, he told himself, to have known the Antarctic
better than to have offered his son the bonus before
their two hundredth whale was dead and actually aboard
the factory ship. A sudden fear took hold of him: that
having given his boy a glimpse of Elysian fields, he
would have, after all, to deny him the opportunity to
walk them.

But they wouldn't give up without a fight. He turned
to the helmsman. "Wake the crew. We'll whale the moment there's light."

* * *

A lovelier or more peaceful morning it would have
been hard to dream of. By 7 A.M. the halo had vanished
from the moon and the flush from the ice, the sea was
aquamarine and smiling, the sky was sapphire, unflawed
by cloud, the warmth of the sun was melting frost
from rigging and spars, and the barometer (in spite of
many a tap) was steady.

But the crew of the *Petrel* were not deceived; they
knew that somewhere beyond the horizon a great storm
was walking the Antarctic. It was the stillness that gave
them warning, a stillness so absolute it could almost be
felt. There was no breath of wind that morning to bring
life to the smile of the sea, no bird in the sky, no seal or
penguin among the floes, and the water which yesterday

had been heavy and rich was now as thin and colourless as if from a tap. Even the shrimplike krill had fled the path of the storm.

And so, it seemed, had the whales. Hour after hour *Petrel* nosed through the sea lanes with never a trace of the longed-for blow. A little after nine o'clock a few faint flecks of white came welling up over the western horizon. The flecks were gossamer-fine at first, and no bigger than the spread of a man's hand, but they thickened and spread.

"Isn't that cirrus, Johan?"

They were sitting outside the galley—the cook and the deckie—sheltered from the bow wind by the flanges of the bridge. The old whaler didn't bother to look up. "Shouldn't wonder."

"First sign of the storm?"

"Aye. But a long way away. . . . Hold the tooth steady, lad!"

Old Johan was carving the ten-inch tooth of a sperm whale into the likeness of a model penguin, and the boy was helping by holding the base of the tooth—though not with his customary attention, for his mind was on other things. After a while Johan laid down his knife. "We've a double deck watch, *and* Thor in the barrel. If a whale blows, we'll not miss it."

"Sorry."

The sun climbed higher, the sea sparkled, and the sky smiled its azure smile; but of the whales which had been so plentiful the day before there was no sign.

"Johan!"

"What is it, lad?" The old whaler knew that the boy was keyed up and wanting reassurance.

"People keep coming back to Antarctica, don't they, year after year?"

"They do."

"Why?"

"Reckon they must like it."

"I know. But *why* do they like it?"

He felt like the man whose child asked, "What is a cow?" and that was easy, but when the child rephrased the question, "Why is a cow?" that wasn't easy at all. For a while he was silent. He could tell the boy of Antarctica's beauty, of the strength of her light, the vividness of her colours and the gemlike glow of her stars; he could describe the far horizons, the solitudes that held no hint of loneliness, and the peace that passed all understanding. Or he could tell him of the comradeship of life in a whalecatcher: fifteen men, all of one company, fighting the storms, the cold and the whales. But the boy was beside him. If he didn't *see* the beauty, if he didn't *feel* the comradeship, what was the use of words? "Reckon," he said slowly, "the Antarctic's like a painting. Some folks see a lot in it, some don't."

"You mean beauty's in the eye of the beholder?"

"That's about it."

"Wonder why it isn't in my eye?"

"It will be, if you wait."

The boy was silent. He told himself that he had no intention of waiting, that when *Petrel* next came south he would be happily studying music in Copenhagen. Yet at the back of his mind was the faintest whisper of doubt —what was it, he wondered, that everyone seemed to see in Antarctica? What was it that brought the whalers back again and again, year after year?

A bell rang softly from the bridge, and *Petrel* heeled over and gathered speed.

The boy was on his feet in a flash. He thought, for one wonderful moment, that they had sighted a whale. But disillusion came fast in the wake of hope; they had only altered course. "Why are we leaving the pack ice, Johan?"

"Whales steer clear o' the pack in a storm."

"Yes, of course . . . When you reckon the storm'll hit us?"

Johan looked at the sky. He didn't like the speed at which the cirrus was spreading, but they had picked up no storm warning—yet—and the glass was high. "Not till the evening, I'd say."

"Hmmm!" Restless, the boy walked to the guardrail and started to scan the sea, segment by segment. He scanned it methodically and for a long time, but there was no more trace of a whale in open water than there had been in the pack. The sun climbed higher. The cirrus spread. His hopes ebbed with the hours.

"Deckie!"

The shout from the radio room came as a relief. He scrambled aft to where the operator was holding a signal out of the window. "Take this to your father. And"—as an afterthought—"you might check the barometer for him."

The boy stuffed the signal into his oilskin pocket and made his way to the barometer. The needle, he was glad to see, still pointed to 30.68, but when he tapped it, it flickered and dropped. He moved on, suddenly afraid, to the bridge. He handed the signal to his father. And as soon as his father unfolded it, he could tell by his face that something was wrong. "What's happening, Dad?"

For a moment Larsen hesitated; then with a shrug, an unhappy disclaimer of events beyond his control, he passed the signal sheet to his son. CYCLOPEAN TO ALL CATCHERS, it read. AT 1030 HOURS JAPANESE FACTORY SHIP NISSHIN MARU II, IN POSITION 500 MILES TO THE WEST-NORTHWEST, REPORTED SEA 9, WIND 11. REPEAT SEA 9,

WIND 11. REPEAT TO PETREL ONLY, BUCK UP WITH YOUR
TWO HUNDREDTH WHALE.

It was hard to believe, as they lay becalmed in a sea
of glass, that only a few hundred miles to the west the
waves were fifty feet high and the wind gusting to close
on a hundred miles an hour. Larsen laid a hand on his
son's shoulder. "Don't give up hope," he said. "The storm
may never come near us."

But the boy was not deceived; like the rest of the
Petrel's crew, he *knew*. He walked to the rail and stared
at the traitorous sea. "Do you wonder," he said after a
while, "I think the Antarctic's cruel?"

Larsen shook his head. "Don't think of it as cruel.
Think of it as a challenge, something that has to be
fought."

The boy made a little gesture of despair. "How can
you fight winds of a hundred miles an hour? And waves
of fifty feet?"

"No one, John, can fight them alone. But a crew can
fight them together."

Something in Larsen's voice made his son look up
quickly. If his father crossed swords with the Antarctic,
that, his instinct told him, would be a battle of giants.
He laid a hand, suddenly anxious, on the sleeve of his
father's oilskins. "Don't do anything silly, Dad. Just for
me."

For a moment their eyes met. Then the boy, as if suddenly embarrassed, was scrambling below.

"The storm may never come near us," Larsen had

said. But he knew in his heart that it would, for the haloed moon and the gathering cloud were portents too explicit to be denied. He was tugged two ways. No whale, no bonus, no Academy for your son, one voice reminded him. But another voice said only a fool would risk his ship and his crew for the sake of a promise. He paced the bridge. He told himself that whalecatchers were tough, that in her ten years in the Antarctic *Petrel* had ridden out any number of storms, and that $10,000 was not to be thrown away without a fight. But it was no good. He knew all the time in his heart that, promise or no promise, he couldn't expose his crew to danger on account of his son, that he must run for shelter, back to the well-screened bay where the factory ship was at anchor. Antarctic storms with waves fifty feet high were not to be taken lightly.

But at least, he thought, we can whale en route. He roughed out a course and a schedule: a course which kept them clear of the shore, and a schedule which allowed them six hours to cover the fifty odd miles to the factory ship. And a little before midday *Petrel* increased speed and swung round to the west-northwest.

The boy had been half expecting this. But not till they were actually on course for *Cyclopean* did the implication of what was happening strike fully home. "Johan, we're giving up!"

"Maybe we'll spot a blow on the way."

The boy held onto the tooth of the sperm like a drowning man to a straw. He found, to his fury, that his eyes were misting over and he was trembling. It was several seconds before he realized that Johan was holding out his knife.

"You care to try shapin' the wing?"

"Thanks." He took the knife gratefully and began with great concentration to pare away at the tooth of the sperm. He worked with care and precision, trying desperately to think of nothing but the exact delineation of the penguin's wing. But it was no good. His eyes kept sliding back to the sea.

After a while Johan said quietly, "Try not to worry, lad. A lot can happen in five or six hours."

At first the words brought comfort. But as morning passed into afternoon and the cirrus gave way to alto-cumulus and the first faint traces of swell came rolling in from the west, the boy grew closer than he cared to admit to tears.

* * *

It came when he was least expecting it, at the moment when he had quite lost hope: the sudden cry from the masthead.

"*Hvalblast!*"

He leapt to his feet. He rushed to the rail. And there, silver against the darkening sky, was the most wonderful sight he had ever seen, the slender and vertical blow of a blue.

* * *

He was the last and greatest of the whales to leave the leads of the pack ice. Other mammals and crustaceans had fled the evening before; but he, conscious of his strength, had lingered behind to feed on the deeply drifting squid. And now, victim of his own self-confidence, he was caught alone and in open sea.

He had no chance of survival. If he ran, the whale-catcher could overhaul him; if he dived, it could hover above him, tracking his movements by asdic until he broke surface. There were no shallows in which he could hide, no bergs round which he could twist and turn, and he had no weapons to fight *Petrel's* Svend Foyn and its hundred-and-eighty-pound harpoon.

"*Hvalblast! Hvalblast!*" A gout of smoke belched black from the whalecatcher's funnel, and she reared up her bow and headed fast for the blow.

The blue fled.

Run north, Larsen willed it, towards the factory ship. But as the blow spurted skyward a second time he saw that their quarry was running south by east, attempting to double back to the shelter of the pack. He gave a grunt of annoyance—the farther they drove the blue from *Cyclopean*, the farther the buoy boats would have to travel to tow it back. He glanced at the sky and was surprised at how much the cloud had thickened in the last half hour; even as he stared at it, a mass of alto-cumulus moved slowly over the sun and the light grew pale. But the storm is coming too late, he thought, to stop us; nothing can stop us now. And the joy of the chase ran warm through his blood like a draught of dog-watch rum. In half an hour, he told himself, the blue will be dead; in a couple of hours the buoy boats will have it in tow; in four hours it will be hauled onto *Cyclopean's* foreplan, and the bonus and all that it means will be ours. He raised his binoculars.

There are few more magnificent sights than a whale at full speed. For twenty to thirty seconds the blue was invisible, swimming flat-out under the surface, then for three to four seconds he rose to blow. First to break water was the great streamlined head, a quarter the length of his body, and at the instant of surfacing a jet of water and stale air shot up to a height of twenty feet, then the head ducked down, and for a moment the great blue-grey bulk of his body, streaming water, lifted clear of the sea—a hundred and fifteen streamlined tons hurtling through the air at the speed of a charging elephant. He re-entered the water smoothly and with hardly a splash, but for all the grace of his diving he left behind him a trail of "footprints," the smoothed-out circles of slick made by the thresh of his tail as it vortexed into the sea.

And in the wake of his "footprints" thundered the *Petrel.* Her stern was awash; smoke was astream from her funnel, and every man of her crew was on deck, clinging to stanchion and companionway, as, tense with excitement, they followed the running of the blue. And most excited of all was the deckie.

The end of the chase was certain as sun after rain. For a while the blue held his own, but after about ten minutes he began to tire and the range to close—thirty

thousand yards, twenty thousand, ten thousand. Then came a check, as the thresh of their screws frightened him into a final and desperate spurt. The spurt, to Larsen's anxiety, went on and on, with every turn of their turbines taking them farther from the factory ship. But no matter how far or how fast you run, he thought, you cannot escape. He checked that the Svend Foyn was loaded, the ropes coiled, the blocks running free, and their position radioed to *Cyclopean;* and by the time he had completed his checks, the blue had been run to exhaustion.

Svend Larsen left the bridge. As he clambered onto the gun platform, the ship became suddenly quiet, hushed and tense as a bull ring at the approach of the moment of truth. He freed the Svend Foyn from its securing stop; he swivelled it this way and that and lined it up on the patch of sea a couple of hundred yards ahead where he expected the blue to break surface. He had barely aligned the cross wires when the great head rose flush on their intersection. He grunted with satisfaction. Asquint through the sights, he could feel little globules of sweat running cold and salt into his eyes; he blinked them away. This, of all the shots he had ever made, was the one that mustn't fail.

Once, twice, three times, at a range of less than eighty yards, the blue heaved slow and helpless out of the sea. The fourth time he surfaced, the Svend Foyn thundered his requiem.

The harpoon flew true. It sliced through the whale's

shoulder and exploded deep in his back. In a froth of incarnadined sea the great creature twisted this way and that, then he dived.

It was the blocks at the masthead now which were the vital links in the chain that held him; they quivered and smoked as a third of a mile of line whipped out of the sheaves; then, as a winch on the foredeck took up the strain, they were depressed to the very foot of the mast. But here, as the line drew taut, they held.

"*Fisk fast!*"

The cry rose jubilant into a darkening sky. And the boy flung his cap so high in the air that the wind caught hold of it and swirled it over the side. But what does it matter, he thought; I need never wear it again.

The blue had not the slightest expectation of life—he was impaled on a hundred-and-eighty-pound hook at the end of a mile of unbreakable line—but he was far from

dead. He fought and flailed with the strength of a herd of elephants, driving the blocks flush against the deck and whipping out another quarter of a mile of line. But his strength was unavailing against the pull of the winch. Slow but sure as the grind of the mills of God the drum revolved, the line wound in, and the great creature was hauled foot by reluctant foot to the surface in a welter of excrement and blood.

The moment he broke water, Larsen gave him the *coup de grâce*. A killer bar (a harpoon with no line attached) smashed into his head. He quivered once, rolled over like a dismasted ship, and came floating belly-up under the whalecatcher's bow.

Larsen looked at him sadly. Only an hour before the blue had been lord of the seas, the mightiest and gentlest of created creatures who in his life had harmed no living animal save the squid and the shrimplike krill; now he was smashed and bleeding and upside down, denied in death the dignity with which he had lived his life. Larsen had been whaling twenty-six years, but still with every kill came the stab of pity; still, after each harpooning, he had to remind himself that the whale's death was not an end but a beginning, that out of each carcass, like sweetness out of the strong, came forth so many pounds of margarine, so many packages of detergent, bars of soap, bottles of lubricant, and blocks of cattle food, so many jars of varnish, cosmetics, glue and ink, so many perfumes, brushes, candles, vitamins and emulsifiers, and so many tons of frozen meat to save the children of the East from death through malnutrition. And out of this particular carcass would come forth something else: the $10,000 reward that would bring such happiness to his son.

He had no need to give orders. While clouds massed dark along the horizon and a snow-wet wind came sighing out of the west, he watched the crew as they prepared the carcass for tow. Within the hour they had cut off and notched its flukes and rigged up an air pipe and pumped a thousand cubic feet of air into the blue's stomach; they were about to flag the carcass with homing aids, when the sky turned dark and the first thin flurry of snow came slanting out of the west.

Larsen glanced at his watch. It was quite a time now since they had radioed their sighting report, and the buoy boats (whose job was to tow the carcass back to *Cyclopean*) should be arriving any moment. But as he raised his binoculars to the horizon it was not the buoy boats which came into focus, it was the swell: the widespread lines of movement spilling silently out of the west. The swell was flat and gentle at the moment, but it wouldn't, Larsen knew, stay flat and gentle for long. He made his way to the radio room. "Any news of the buoy boats?"

The operator shook his head. Atmospherics, he said, were bad, and he was having difficulty in keeping the factory ship in contact. All he could be certain of was that both his sighting and killing reports had been received and understood.

Larsen returned to the bridge. He could picture the scene in the horseshoe bay where *Cyclopean* lay at anchor, the buoy boats ascurry hither and thither to tow in the carcasses, their task given added urgency by the ending of the season and the approach of the storm. Several times in the next half hour he raised his binoculars to the horizon; any moment, he told himself, the buoy boats would come swimming into focus. But the minutes passed and the only change in the horizon was a darkening and thickening of cloud. He was about to call the buoy boats direct—a procedure that was frowned on except in emergency—when his son came scrambling onto the bridge.

"Captain Sandberg, Dad. On the radio."

He hurried aft, wondering—it was unusual for the master of *Cyclopean* to have time to talk to an individual skipper. In the radio room he clamped on his earphones, grimacing at the crackle of static. "Larsen speaking."

"Svend! Roald Sandberg here. I'll not beat about the bush. There's the hell of a storm building up. I daren't risk the boats for a tow of sixty miles."

The blow was all the crueller for being so totally unexpected. For a moment he was bereft of words.

"Can you hear me, Svend?"

"Yes, I can hear you."

"I'm sorry. Your two hundredth whale, wasn't it?"

"Yes."

"God knows I'd like to help. But I daren't risk the boats off a lee shore."

"I know how it is." The words came automatically, a seaman's acceptance of authority.

"Reckoned you'd understand. Best I can do is make you a promise: if the weather clears in time, your whale will be picked up first. Are you still with it?"

"Yes."

"Better leave it and clear the shore. The storm looks a real bastard."

"Thanks for the tip."

An awkward pause, then: "I'm sorry, Svend. Look after yourself." A crackle of static and the receiver went dead.

He took off his earphones and walked slowly out of the radio room. He was defeated, and there was nothing he could do about it. He knew very well that by the time the storm had blown itself out, the season would be closed and it would be too late to bring in his whale and claim the bonus. Anger built up in him, not with the Antarctic, for whose caprices he ought to have been prepared, but with himself, for having taken too much for granted. He could hear his son, whistling happily as he helped to get ready the evening meal, and the knowledge of what he would have to tell him was like the turn of a knife in his heart. But when a thing has got to be done, he told himself, it is best done quickly. He made his way to the galley.

When the boy saw the look on his father's face, the whistling stopped.

Larsen broke the new as gently as he could, although the blow, in fact, was not the sort that it was possible to soften. He was half prepared for recriminations or tears. But his son hadn't cried since coming aboard and he had no intention of starting now; he simply walked to the rail and stared out at the darkening sea.

Larsen longed to comfort him, to tell him he loved

him, to prove to him that he cared, but the things that he felt in his heart he wasn't able to put into words. After a while he walked across to his son and put an arm round his shoulders. "Sorry, lad . . . But we'll get the bonus one year. And when we get it, it'll be yours."

The boy looked up at his father and tried to smile. "Thanks anyway, Dad," he said, "for trying."

* * *

It was the smile and the thank you that did it, that drove Svend Larsen the one last step beyond the limit of prudence.

The idea had come to him while he was speaking to Sandberg. He had rejected it then; so why, he asked himself, was he worrying at it now, like a dog agnaw at the bone it knows to be meatless but cannot leave? It was the tow of the S.S. *Sheathbill* that he couldn't get out of his mind. *Sheathbill* was a catcher which, in the 1950's, had become the talk of the whaling fleets by towing a blue whale for forty miles through gradually thickening pack ice. (Whalecatchers are usually used to kill rather than tow, but they can, if the need arises, shackle onto a carcass and drag it along behind them—though Larsen had never heard of a catcher dragging its whale for sixty miles through a Force Nine storm.) He was weighing the odds—in one scale all that the bonus would mean to his son, in the other the risk to his ship and his crew—when the mate came clambering onto the bridge.

"What is it, Torstein?"

The big whaler, onetime cruiser-weight champion of the Antarctic fleets, cleared his throat. "One or two of us have been thinking, Svend."

"Yes?"

"Do you remember the old *Sheathbill*?"

"I do."

"Well, we reckon what she could do, we can do."

"*Sheathbill* hadn't to tow through a storm."

"And we haven't to tow through ice. . . . Anyway, Svend, the crew want you to know: we'll be real disappointed if you don't give it a try."

He was moved more deeply than he cared to admit. And yet he hesitated. For a moment he had the sensation of being trapped, of having been driven step by step into a position he should never have been in. But as he looked at his son the moment passed. He checked his watch. They had thirty-two hours till the end of the season, thirty-two hours to cover sixty miles. In good weather it would have been child's play; in the storm it would be work for men. But they had a very definite chance.

"Helmsman!" He turned to the man at the wheel. "Lay us alongside the carcass, bow to tail."

He walked to the guardrail, to where his son stood staring out to sea. "We'll tow the whale back," he said, "ourselves."

The sky, as if in mockery, turned suddenly dark, and a snow squall, thick and sharp as a flurry of arrows, heeled *Petrel* almost onto her beam.

* * *

Speed and care were the requisites of success. Speed, because they needed to break the back of the tow before the storm built up to its climax; care, because a badly tied lashing could cost them their whale, and a badly chosen course their lives.

"Torstein! Jamie!" At Larsen's shout the mate and the chief engineer came scrambling onto the bridge. "We'll tow him ourselves. Two bracelets over the flukes, double lashings, and three thicknesses of canvas."

"Right. Do we tow to port or starboard?"

He hesitated. To port, the carcass would ride awkwardly, exposed to the full lash of the storm; to starboard, it would be sheltered, but it would tend to pull their head inshore and drag them onto the pack ice. Safety, he told himself, was more important than comfort. "Secure to port. I'll do the plot."

As mate and engineer disappeared down the for'd hatch, he took a quick look at the weather. What he saw was not reassuring. There was no trace now of the sun or the azure sky. Instead was a low-slung canopy of cloud, a cheerless grey, streaked here and there with patches of black as snow squalls emptied like ink into a rising sea. But as long as we keep clear of the shore, he thought, there'll be more discomfort than danger. He turned his attention to the plot.

A mistake here would be fatal: a track too far to seaward and they would never get back to the factory ship in time, a track too close inshore and they would be swept up and crushed in the disintegrating fields of ice. He studied his charts, cursing the promontory of Cape Herschel which jutted out like an angry fang across their line of advance. They would have to stand seaward first, till they had weathered the cape, then cut back inshore to the bay where the factory ship was at anchor. He laid off a dog-leg track, which he hoped was a fair compromise between the need for speed and the need for safety. He measured it, and it totalled sixty-nine miles. That's thirty hours' tow, he thought, at two and a quarter knots. But we can do better than two and a quarter knots to start with. He roughed out a schedule:

3 hours towing at	5	knots	= 15 miles
3　〃　　〃　　〃	4	〃	= 12　〃
3　〃　　〃　　〃	3	〃	= 9　〃
10　〃　　〃　　〃	2	〃	= 20　〃
10　〃　　〃　　〃	1½	〃	= 15　〃
29 hours			71 miles

This was the goal they must aim at; if they could keep to this, his son would be sure of a place at the Academy.

The thud of the blue on their bow brought him back to the present.

The whale rode quietly beside them, sheltered from waves whose crests were now flecked with occasional ribands of white and a wind sufficiently strong to make a small but continuous moan in the rigging. Twin bracelets, padded with canvas, had been slip-knotted round its tail, so that the more it tried to tug free, the more tightly it was held, and the bracelets had been secured inboard with double lashings via hawses and slips. It looked as though catcher and whale were riveted one to another by bonds that not even the most frenetic storm could break. But Laren was taking no chances. Not till he had inspected every lashing and chain did he give the order to sever the forerunner—the rope that had held the blue in place while the bracelets were being made fast.

This was the moment of danger.

"Clear the decks! All hands under cover!" As the tannoy blared loud and discordant above the moan of a rising wind, the mate picked up his flensing knife and walked to the rail. The arc lamps had just been switched on; and thrown into sharp relief by their glare, he looked

like an actor spotlit on the stage for some spectacular finale.

Three times *Petrel* rolled rhythmically in the swell, and three times the forerunner ran out to an easy degree of tension. Torstein nodded with satisfaction, and as the fourth roll gathered momentum, his knife flashed down. But the fourth roll was steeper than those that had gone before and a fraction earlier; at the crucial moment the blue jerked away from the catcher, and the rope, at the second of impact, pulled suddenly taut. Severed under pressure, its tip whipped back, wickedly, straight at the mate.

He flung himself to the deck. The forerunner snaked over his head, scoured a groove out of a bollard, and wrapped itself, with a crack that was heard in the engine room, round a bar of the guardrail. The guardrail, a half-inch cast-iron rod, was wrenched out of its socket and tossed, smoking, the width of the deck.

"Torstein!" Larsen was beside him before *Petrel* had straightened out of her roll.

"All right. I'm used to ducking punches!" He got to his feet slowly, rubbing his head and flexing his arms and legs as if to reassure himself that he was all of a piece. "My mistake." He picked his cap and knife out of the scuppers. "Reckon I was lucky."

"Very lucky!" Larsen ran his fingers over the mate's cap. Its peak was sliced off, clean as grain by a reaper.

They looked at each other as the narrowness of the escape struck home, and Larsen's thoughts were taken back to his first season and the mate who hadn't been as quick on his feet as Torstein—he had died of shock as they tried to tighten a tourniquet round what was left of his legs. "Don't do that again," he said slowly. "I don't like my crew losing their heads."

He walked to the bridge. He stared at the blue in the way that a boxer might stare at the adversary with whom he expects to be in the ring for quite a while. "Helmsman! Steer oh-one-eight degrees."

As the whalecatcher swung into wind, she became suddenly alive. For the last hour the swell rolling in on her quarter had been lifting her up in a not ungentle corkscrew, while the carcass had ridden comparatively quiet in her lee. It was different now, with the swell crashing into her bow and the blue aflail at its lashings as if resurrected to life.

It was five-thirty as they got under way. Sunset was not for another four hours, but already the sky was dark, the occasional wave was slopping over their gunwhale, and in sheltered places on the foredeck little pools of water were solidifying to ice. And the barometer read 29.2, falling.

* * *

On deck, violence and cold: the wind gusting to fifty knots, the sea rising, the snow squalls thickening, and the crew rigging life and guide lines from capstan to mizzen. In the galley, comfort and warmth: the aromatic hiss of saucepans, and steam acoil like incense out of the ovens as the cook and the deckie got ready the evening meal—

great mounds of sausages, tinned peas and mashed potatoes.

"That enough?" The boy held out a two-gallon buck-
et, full to the brim of potatoes peeled and sliced.

"Best have another couple o' pounds."

"Johan! We'll burst!"

"A crew fights best on a full stomach."

For a while they worked in silence, most of the time
swaying instinctively to the movement of the ship, but
having every now and then to steady themselves as *Petrel*
rolled more steeply than usual. As he peeled the last few
pounds of potatoes, it came to the boy that he was having
to grab the stanchions for support with increasing frequency.

"Storm's getting worse."

"Aye. An' it'll be worse still before it's better."

By 7 P.M. the meal was simmering in the ovens, and they had nothing to do but wait.

"Johan!" The boy's voice was thoughtful.

Hmmm?"

"Don't the crew *mind* my getting the bonus?"

"Mind? Why should we mind? It was our idea in the first place."

"I know. But aren't things different now? I mean, the ship's getting bashed about, the crew are getting bashed about—Torstein's nearly been killed—and it's all because of me."

Johan shook his head. "You've no need, lad, to feel like that. The crew are right happy to try and win the bonus for you. And besides, 'twouldn't matter *who* was gettin' the bonus—say it was your father, or Torstein, or me—the crew would still be wantin' to earn it. That's the point about a crew. They pull together. Like a family."

"Makes me feel sort of small."

"Ah! That's maybe the start to your growin' big!"

Silence, except for the mounting cacophony of the storm: the shriller whine of the wind, the sharper crack of their bows as they fell off the crests of waves that were becoming too steep to ride, the drumming crescendo on their superstructure of hard-packed granules of snow, and the thousand and one little groans and complaints of a ship fighting for her life. The boy scratched his ear: "You mean if I feel small, I'm starting to grow up?" His voice was puzzled.

"Reckon that's so."

Johan was checking the temperature of the pans when *Petrel*, caught by an unexpected shift of wind and sea, slewed suddenly broadside on. In an instant, weighed down by the bulk of the blue, she rolled sickenly, guard-rail under.

In the saloon cutlery and mugs smashed into the fiddles; on deck the door of the rope locker burst open and festoons of nylon and wire shot over the side, and in the galley scalding water slopped viciously out of the pans. Johan, who had missed being burned by a hairs-breadth, stared at the pans in disbelief. They were proof against overflowing in rolls of up to forty degrees.

"Johan!" The boy's voice was frightened.

"Hold on. She's over again."

A second time scalding water came sluicing out of the pans. But not so much. For the helmsman now was haul-ing round the whalecatcher's head, and by the time the next wave hit her she was bow into sea and the danger had passed.

"Did you say the storm would get worse?" The boy's face was white.

"Never mind the storm. Get dryin' the deck."

They mopped and squeegeed away the water, keeping a wary eye on the ovens. Then, when the galley was back to normal, the boy stacked fifteen plates for warming while Johan brewed up the tea.

It was seven-thirty as the crew came together for what, as many of them guessed, was to be their last hot meal for forty-eight hours. They came into the saloon thankfully, like storm-tossed birds to shelter, blinking in the strong white light, shedding oilskins, stamping their feet and rubbing their hands. They sat down with grunts of relief, ate hungrily, and talked of anything but the storm—for this was a time to relax and as far as possible forget.

But they weren't able to forget for long. The meal was barely half over when Larsen, his oilskins white with salt, came in with news of the tow. "We've been on course two hours"—even in the shelter of the saloon he had to shout to make himself heard—"and we've made twelve miles. That's good." He laid a hand on the chief engineer's shoulder. "Keep this up, and by midnight the tow'll be cracked."

"So'll my boilers!"

They laughed. And the boy, as he watched them, was filled with a sudden happiness. All this, he thought, they are doing for me. They're fighting the blue and the storm; they're straining their engines, risking their deck plates and even their lives—and all to win me a place at the Academy. They can't think so badly of me after all. For the first time since leaving the Falkland Islands he felt almost as if he belonged. It was ironic, he told himself, that the very battle which would enable him to quit whaling should make him realize for the first time a little of what he might be missing by giving it up.

The meal was nearly over when the door of the saloon swung open a second time and Torstein reeled in, in a flurry of wind and snow. He sat next to Larsen, and the two of them, oblivious to their food, began to talk anxiously. Something, the boy realized, was wrong; something, to judge from his father's expressions, serious.

Larsen banged the table for silence. "We're icing up." His voice had a touch of anxiety. "A couple of inches on the foredeck, a layer on the boat deck, and a crust round the flying bridge and the chains. Now I want two working parties, turn and turn about, a pair for'd and a pair aft."

They knew what was wanted—men with ten-pound hammers to break up and dislodge the ice as it formed on superstructure and deck. Cold, unpleasant work, but work that had to be done, or the ice would build up to a solid, top-heavy sheet, weighing them down and eventuaaly turning them turtle. After a deal of bantering and manuvering (which Larsen knew better than to hurry) the brothers Carl and Bengt volunteered to make up one pair. But they still needed another. The boy jumped suddenly to his feet. "I'll do a shift."

He's too light, Larsen thought, and he'll tire too easily. He was about to shake his head, when Johan pushed back his chair. "The deckie and I," he said, "will make the other pair."

Skipper and cook had been whaling together for fifteen years, and they trusted each other's judgment. "Right." Larsen's voice was casual, but his eyes didn't leave old Johan's face. "A two-hour shift. And remember: once overboard in a sea like this, there'll be no picking anyone up."

He was too excited at first to be frightened. It was a Big Adventure: the extra clothes, the spiked boots, the loops to secure him to the life lines, the advice, the warnings and the last hot drink before they left the comfort and warmth of the saloon. But once on deck, the Adventure was metamorphosed to nightmare.

It was the wind that shocked him most. The second they opened the door of the saloon, it clawed at them like an animal, smashing them against the superstructure, driving the snow into their eyes and sucking the breath out of their mouths. For a couple of minutes they huddled in the comparative shelter of the bridge, getting their breath and their bearings; then Carl and Bengt began to work their way aft.

Johan looked at the deckie and saw that he was afraid. He neither blamed him nor judged him, simply wondered how to help him—whether to give him time to conquer his fear or work to drug it?

The boy shifted impatiently. "Let's make a start, Johan." His words were lost in the storm, but not their meaning.

Clinging to the guidelines and choosing their moment between waves, they slithered for'd.

The foredeck was a solid sheet of ice, except for a small area immediately beneath the gun mounting which was protected from wind and spray; here they were able to stand in comparative shelter. The boy unslung his hammer and began to prod at the ice, but Johan was not to be hurried. "Have a look round, lad. Get your bearings."

The boy moistened his lips and forced himself to take stock of a world which in the last few hours had darkened and closed in until it consisted of two things only, the storm and the *Petrel*.

The storm covered the face of the earth, and no part of the earth was visible that was not storm. Great waves, a mile and a quarter from crest to crest, came thundering in endless succession out of the dark. Each, as it neared *Petrel*, towered high above her; each, it seemed to the boy, must engulf her utterly. Yet always she rose, climbed the steepening incline, hung for a moment on the crest, and then plunged in a sickening breath-catching swoop into the pit of the following trough. Above the waves the sky hung low and grey, torn ribbons of cloud, cataracting snow, streaming past as if in the wake of an explosion. And everywhere was the wind. It was the wind that was worst of all, a continual roar, rising now and then to a high-pitched shriek of malevolence as its fiercer gusts ripped off the crests of the waves and flung them horizontally over the sea.

And in the center of the storm, the *Petrel*. Though it still needed an hour to sunset, her riding and navigation lights were aglow, and an arc lamp high on her mast cut a great circle of whiteness out of the dark—a circle that was never still, but shifted with every movement of the ship, now spotlighting the foredeck, now the boat deck, now throwing into sharp relief a flurry of snow and now a great wall of advancing sea. When the light of the arc swung for'd to where the boy and the cook were standing, it delineated the bows with nightmare clarity: the dark-green sheen of the ice, the white of the spindrift, and the silver of icicles festooning the rails and the flying bridge.

Johan cupped his hands to the boy's ear. "You checked the life lines? And the bollards you can hang on to?"

He nodded.

"Ready to start?"

He nodded again.

It needed a few minutes to eight o'clock as they began to hammer away the ice. It was difficult work. The deck canted this way and that; spray smashed into them like the jet of a fireman's hose; waves sluiced green through the guardrail, knocking them off their feet, while the wind sucked the breath from their lungs and threatened any moment to pick them up and smash them senseless into bollard or capstan. If they hadn't been secured to the guidelines, they would have been overboard in the first five minutes.

Johan watched the boy carefully, noting with satisfaction how he used his hammer with one hand and held tight to line or rail with the other, but noting, too, that he had neither the strength nor the experience to make much impression on the ice. For the ice was recalcitrant. In some places, where it had formed slowly, it was tough and rubbery and needed several blows before it was dislodged; in other places a great mound of it would distintegrate at a touch, so that the hammer jarred through to the deck. It took them half an hour to work from gun mounting to galley, clearing en route the ratlines, guardrails and flying bridge, and by the time they had finished, a new layer of ice had formed in their wake, as tough and resilient as the old. They sheltered awhile in the lee of the gun mounting, getting back their breath, then they began all over again.

From the bridge Svend Larsen watched them. Each time the sea and the spray swept over his son, he flinched and closed his eyes. As time passed he realized he was flinching and closing his eyes with increasing frequency. He cursed—much use he was to his ship with his eyes shut! He lurched to the back of the bridge and forced himself to study the plot.

They had been towing for the last few hours at six knots, which meant they were ahead of schedule. But the seas had now built up to such a pitch of malevolence that at the speed they were hitting *Petrel* they were threatening to carry away both working parties and blue; for each gigantic comber, as it went foaming past, tugged and tore at the carcass like the teeth of a great animal, so that even from inside the bridge Larsen could hear the tortured shriek of slips and chains grinding together, as a man grinds his teeth in agony under a strain too terrible to be endured.

He rang for four knots.

At their reduced speed the blue rode easier and the seas didn't break so frequently over their bow. After

a while he glanced at his watch: nine-thirty. Only another half hour till the working parties changed over.
He hoped that now they were riding more steadily, his
son would survive the rest of the shift without getting
swept off his feet.

Johan hoped so too—but he wouldn't have liked to
put money on it. He kept close to the boy, well aware
of the lack of resilience in his legs and the unco-
ordinated swings of his hammer, but aware, too, that for
all his exhaustion he had the sense to keep hold of the
life lines. As they paused for a moment in the shelter of
the Svend Foyn, he again cupped his hands to the boy's
ear. "How you feelin'?"

"Fine."

"Okay for a last half hour?"

The boy nodded.

"Right. Stay 'longside o' me."

John Larsen was determined not to give up. He hadn't
backed out of a job since joining *Petrel* and he certainly wasn't starting now. It's my whale, he told himself,
and I must pull my weight getting it back. He wiped the
spray from his eyes and the salt from his mouth, took a
grip on the life line, and swung his hammer at the ice.
The deck canted; he missed the ice and hit the capstan,
and a tingling jar ran up his arm from wrist to elbow.
He swung again, but the backwash threw him off
balance and the blow fell short.

"Hold on!"

As his hand tightened on the guideline, a great wall
of water hit him flush on the chest, knocking the air out

of his lungs and smashing him into the capstan. He thought for a second that *Petrel* was foundering, then as suddenly as it had come the water was gone and Johan beside him was unconcernedly knocking away the ice. He swung his hammer again and again, automatically, sometimes making contact, sometimes missing, but always, by an innate sense of self-preservation, holding tight to the life lines. His head ached, and his left knee, which had been bruised on a bollard, was swollen and sore. But he was determined not to give up. Time, after a while, lost all meaning; he might have been hammering away for half the night when he heard, as if from another world, Johan shouting at him, again and again. But not till the old whaler took him by the hand and led him to the door of the saloon did he realize that the second working party were already on deck and hammering away at the ice. . . .

He fell asleep as Johan was helping him off with his boots. He didn't wake as they carried him below or as they laid him out on his bunk. Splayed out like a starfish, he slept the sleep of the physically exhausted, his face flushed pink in the warmth of the cabin like the face of a very young child.

But there was no sleep that night for the crew.

Turn and turn about, as the storm built up to its climax they cleared the ice and kept watch in engine room and bridge. And at last—according to the plot— *Petrel* drew level with the fanglike promontory of Cape Herschel.

But could the plot be trusted?

For the last hour Larsen had been trying to check their position by radar or radio, but both echo and transmission were too distorted by the storm to offer him more than the roughest guide. Cape Herschel might have been anything from five to ten miles to starboard; the factory ship might have been on any bearing from 045° to 060°.

By eleven-fifteen *Petrel* was past the point where, according to slide rule and log, she ought to have altered course. Yet Larsen gave no orders but stood staring, puzzled, at the changing pattern of the sea. Up to now the storm had built up slowly, almost casually, like a giant unveiling a strength that he knows to be limitless; but in the last quarter of an hour the waves had taken on a sudden viciousness; they had grown steeper, closer together, and alive with an indefinable menace. It was as if the water was shoaling.

He checked the plot. He got Torstein to double-check it. And they both worked out their position as well clear of the shoals that jutted out from the tip of Herschel. Yet the waves, unmistakably, were piling up.

Torstein scratched his head. "What did you lay off for the wind?"

"Seventy knots."

"Must be more!"

They stared at each other. They couldn't believe it at first. But as they rechecked their calculations, they realized it was the only possible answer—that they were being driven inshore by a wind of more than a hundred miles an hour.

"Helmsman!" Larsen's voice was sharp. "Forty degrees to port."

Petrel crabbed round, awkwardly but safe. Then, beam on to wind and sea, she started to roll.

She rolled sickeningly, tumbling off the crests in a turmoil of spume, and wallowing in the troughs to within a hairsbreadth of turning turtle. Larsen rang for a knot and a half. The reduction in speed made them ride a little more easily—but not much. He doubled the lookouts, put an extra man on the wheel, and called *Cyclopean* for an estimate of the wind.

It was some time before he could tell if their change of course was taking them out of danger, for with *Petrel* rolling rather than pitching, it was hard to gauge the comparative steepness of the waves. But after a while he judged by the smoother movement of the ship that the combers were flattening and spacing out. But he was taking no chances. It was close on midnight before, convinced at last that they were clear of the shoals of Herschel, he turned onto their final leg, the last thirty-odd miles that would take them, God willing, to *Cyclopean*.

Soon after they had settled on course, the radio operator came onto the bridge with the factory ship's estimate of the wind. Larsen smoothed out the signal. CYCLOPEAN, he read, TO PETREL. WIND 80 KNOTS, GUSTING 100, RISING. IF YOU ARE WHERE I THINK YOU ARE, CUT YOUR TOW AND MAKE FOR OPEN SEA.

"Did you acknowledge this?"

The operator smiled. "I wasn't born yesterday!"

Larsen nodded. "If they go on calling, send: 'Sorry, I cannot read you.' "

He held the signal lightly between forefinger and thumb, walked to the rail, and watched it disappear into the storm. An order never received couldn't be disobeyed.

He wedged himself into the least wind-swept corner of the bridge and stared at the great seas rolling endlessly out of the night. He was tired and cold, and the perpetual roar of the storm (like a giant river in spate) made him physically and mentally bemused; but the knowledge his crew were behind him brought comfort. With a crew like mine, he thought, it will take more than a hundred-knot gale to make us call off the tow. But as the hours passed, the seas, as if to disprove him, increased in fury. Soon there was only one word to describe them: mountainous; great ranges of water, their lower slopes dark as forests, their upper slopes white as snow, and with spray astream from their crests like pennants of storm-tossed cloud. And even more terrifying than the waves was the wind, the wind that with increasing frequency ripped off the wave crests and drove them horizontally over the sea. These were the worst moments of all, when *Petrel* in the path of a great avalanche of water reeled and staggered as hundreds of tons of spindrift sluiced green the width of her deck. It was at these moments that a drum began to beat softly in Larsen's head: "Cut the tow, cut the tow." He checked the barometer. It read 28.6, and it was still falling.

After a while he realized that someone was tugging at his shoulder. It was Johan, trying to preserve the remnants of a mugful of cocoa.

"Ah!" He flexed his fingers and stamped his feet and blew the steam off his mug. "How's John?"

"Asleep in his cabin."

"Best place for him."

Johan nodded. "You know what he said before he fell asleep? 'When it's my turn for another shift, promise to wake me.' "

"And did you promise?"

"He was asleep before I could answer!"

"Just as well." Larsen walked leaden-footed to the plot and laid off their position. "Twenty-three hours and fifty minutes," he said, "to go, twenty-nine miles to cover."

"Looks like we're going to make it."

"So long as nothing goes wrong."

The words were hardly out of his mouth when the bracelet parted.

3.

Tuesday, April 8th

The chain flew back into its hawse only a couple of feet above the bunk where the boy was sleeping.

Startled, he jerked up, cracking his head on the bulkhead. He saw the walls of the cabin tilting, tilting and not coming back, and thought that he must be going to faint; not till he found himself in a heap on the floor did he realize the angle of the walls was no illusion, that *Petrel* was heeled over at an angle of more than forty degrees. Panic swept over him. They were foundering, and he trapped helpless below. But as the seconds passed and the walls held steady and there was no great inrush of sea, he began instinctively to struggle into his life jacket. Within a minute of the tow parting he was on deck, staring at a scene that pricked up the hair on the nape of his neck.

Petrel was canted over so sharply that her guardrail

was under water and the top of her mast was all but feathering the sea. Her deck was in shadow, but the great waves as they swept onto her were thrown into terrifying clarity by the light of the arc. And wavering through the light of the arc was a riband of green, the one shaft of colour to irradiate the night. The boy stared, half mesmerized, at the band of green. It was several seconds before he realized what it was: the beam from their riding light, refracted *under* water into a glittering skein of viridescence. But even as he stared at it, the greenness wavered and broke as *Petrel* lifted onto a more even keel.

The sea let her go reluctantly—like quicksand robbed of the victim whose fate had seemed certain. But gradually, as she came up into wind, her list diminished, she shook herself free of the water and lost her terrifying lack of resilience.

The boy took courage. And as soon as he realized they were not, after all, about to founder, he remembered the tow. He saw to his amazement that the blue was still with them, but held now by only the single bracelet and slip. And how long could a single bracelet and slip withstand the wrench of the storm?

He knew enough about whaling to realize there were three things they could do. They could cut the carcass adrift; they could carry on towing with the one bracelet, or they could try to secure another.

The first was the way of defeat. And they were not, the boy could tell, going to take it—for if his father had intended to cut the tow, he would have cut it at once, when *Petrel* had been within a hairsbreadth of turning turtle. The second was the way of delusion. For if one bracelet out of a pair had parted, one by itself would certainly do the same. The third was the way of danger; for passing a bracelet round the tail of the blue would be hazardous in the extreme, since waves and flukes alike could sweep a working party into the sea before they had time to cry out. And yet this, the boy could see, was what they were going to try. He was filled once again with a sudden elation: they were risking everything for him, even their lives. And mixed up this time with his elation was a sentiment he had never experienced before: a sense of belonging, of being not so much an individual as part of a ship's company, one of the little shipload of men who were pitting their skill, ingenuity and courage against the worst that Antarctica could throw at them. He slid eagerly down the foredeck to the group of whalers stopping down a new bracelet with inch-and-a-half cordage. "Can I help?"

The mate shook his head. "Keep clear of the deck, lad."

He wanted to lend a hand, but the crew, it seemed, wanted him out of the way. He was deflated, and yet he could see the justice in it—for everyone else knew what to do without being told, and a crisis was no time to start explanations. Frustrated and chastened, he took shelter in the doorway of the saloon. From here he could watch what he couldn't take part in—the passing of a second bracelet round the tail of the blue.

The scene was like some macabre ballet played out to a frenzied cacophony of storm. Groups of whalers moved in and out of the circle of arc light, strengthening life lines, wrapping canvas round bracelet and chain, and securing a second tail strop to the capstan. They worked in silence, one moment in darkness, the next, as the mast tilted forward, in bright magnesium light; their gestures were dramatic, now turning their faces from the lash of spindrift, now straining at bracelet or hawser, and now jerked down the life lines like so many marionettes. But the waves that broke onto the foredeck and swept them off their feet were rare now. For *Petrel* had reversed course and was running with wind and sea on her quarter. Heading in this direction, the blue was sheltered from the blundgeoning of the sea, and there was little danger of a "milestone" (their bows riding high and crashing down from the crest of a wave). But there *was* another danger, for with the wind behind them they were heading back into the shoals of Herschel.

As the boy stared down the foredeck, the whalers dispersed, leaving only two figures in the circle of light: the men whose job was to pass the bracelet over the tail. The boy had time to recognize one of them—Torstein— then the figures were lost in shadow. But a moment later, as the light of the arc came pouring back, he caught sight of the face of the other. It was Johan.

* * *

When a man has given his life to one calling, how can you tell him he is too old to go on with it? If the man is your friend, you cannot.

When *Petrel* was running smooth with the sea behind her, Larsen called for volunteers to secure the second bracelet. He called for volunteers because the job was dangerous: a pair of whalers, knee-deep in water, having to lean over the guardrail, unreeve the eye of the bracelet and shackle it to the tail strop. A slip, a milestone or a blow from the flukes, and they would be swept lifeless into the storm. A good number of whalers stepped forward to volunteer, but there was no doubt as to who stepped forward first—Torstein and Johan.

Torstein, as mate, was the obvious man for the job. But Johan, at fifty-seven, was the oldest aboard by almost a decade, and as *Petrel's* cook he had been excluded for years from the more dangerous work on deck. Larsen would have liked to pretend that he hadn't seen him, but as the old whaler stepped forward their eyes met, and he knew that if he chose anyone else, Johan would know he had been passed over, and why.

"Torstein and Johan." He pushed his doubts to the back of his mind. The old man, he told himself, was strong and experienced; he could do the job as well as anyone. "Be careful," he said, "and take your time."

He said, "take your time," but he knew, and Torstein and Johan knew, that they hadn't much time to play with. For with the wind and sea behind them, they were running fast into shoal water.

As he steadied the helm Larsen wished he had four pairs of eyes: one pair for the waves sweeping in from astern, one pair for the compass card, one pair for Torstein and Johan, and one long-sighted pair to give warning of shoaling ahead. He called for flares to be fired over their bow, at two-minute intervals.

The whoosh of the first rocket was drowned by the storm, and the first the crew knew of its firing was the three great balls of light that mushroomed out of the cloud. The balls of light were swirled away fast, but not before they had spotlit, way ahead, the white of breaking waves and the glint of ice. Larsen's lips tightened. He turned, as if in supplication, to Torstein and Johan. If they didn't fix the tow fast, it would never be fixed at all.

But even as he watched, Torstein, leaning over the rail, unreeved the eye; and Johan, quickly and accurately, pushed through the last link of the chain and shackled it to the tail strop.

Larsen wiped the spray from his eyes. They had done it. He'd give them a couple of minutes to haul the bracelet tight, then reverse course.

The wave hit them as he had only one hand on the wheel and half his attention on Torstein and Johan. It slewed them sideways, and green water came pouring over their stern—only a little green water, but enough to knock Johan off his feet.

He was turning to the mate, relaxed in the satisfaction of a job well done, when the deck canted awkwardly, and before he could tighten his grip on the life line the sea knocked his legs from under him and swept him against the rail. He would have been all right if it hadn't been for the broken bracelet, the five hundred pounds of cast-iron chain which wrapped itself whiplike round his legs. Pain knifed through his kneecap; the deck turned red, and a great wave of darkness swept out of the sea and over his eyes.

The boy saw it all.

"Johan!" His hand flew to his mouth; his teeth clenched tighter and tighter till blood ran warm through his fingers. Then he was rushing to the rail.

They secured the old man's shoulders to a life line, then lifted the bracelet, very carefully, away from his legs. At the sight of what was under the bracelet

Torstein's lips tightened. "A stretcher. Hurry." But the brothers Carl and Bengt were already scrambling with it to the rail.

Torstein had hoped that Johan would stay unconscious until they had carried him below; but as they were struggling to lift him onto the stretcher, spume drove into his face and his eyes flickered open.

"Lie still, Johan."

"I'm all right." He was about to heave himself up when he saw his leg. Tibia and fibula were protruding through the skin below the kneecap like the broken masts of a wreck. He lay still. His face was grey and beaded with sweat, and he was breathing fast.

Larsen pushed through to him. "Don't move, Johan. We'll get you below." He unsealed the first aid box. He was feeling in it for the tablets of morphine when a wave sluiced green into *Petrel's* waist. He grabbed at the rail for support, missed, and cannoned into Torstein. Both in an instant were swept off their feet. In his anxiety not to fall on Johan, Larsen dropped the first aid box, and the sea picked it up and lifted it smoothly and cleanly over the side. He cursed. There were, he knew, other and smaller first aid kits (in the ship's boats and survival packs) but none that contained the pain-killing morphine. A second wave came foaming up to his thighs. *Petrel's* pitching, he realized, had suddenly steepened. He peered over the bow, and as the next group of flares came swinging out of cloud, he cursed again. For the water ahead was shoaling.

He grabbed Torstein. "No time to get him below. Into the saloon with him. Quick." He ran for the bridge. God help them, he thought, if I have to turn before they get clear of the deck. As he took the wheel, a familiar drumbbeat began to throb through his head: "Cut the tow, cut the tow; you'll get round smoother and faster if only you'll cut the tow." But he shut his mind to the warning and shouted for flares every thirty seconds. He listened. Was it imagination or was there now another sound over and above the cacophony of the storm: a deeper, more menacing roar, the thunder of giant waves as they pounded themselves to death on the edge of the ice? The flares blossomed out. He peered anxiously into their circles of light, and as they plummeted into the sea, he caught his breath. Less than a mile ahead was a continuous wall of spray flung high into the air, a place of death where the sea and the ice joined battle.

A quick look aft, and he saw they had lifted Johan onto the stretcher and were struggling with him towards the saloon. Somehow he must delay his turn until they had got him bedded down.

The flares were falling in continuous succession now, drifting out of the cloud and tumbling in pools of liquid gold onto the ice. The scene that they spotlit had a terrifying beauty, a beauty which, as they were swept towards it, increased in clarity and detail with every second. Soon they could hear the thunder of breaking waves and see the great blocks of ice, hard as adamant, being pulverized into fragments, tossed a hundred feet into the air, and flung back onto the quaking morass of the ice field. Out of the corner of his eye Larsen saw the stretcher being carried through the door of the saloon. I'll give them half a minute, he thought, then turn. He stared ahead, watching for shoals, judging the depth of the sea by *Petrel's* uneasy corkscrew and pitch. When he had counted twenty seconds, he glanced astern, and thinking that the seas in their wake looked for the moment comparatively innocuous, he reached for the tannoy. "Hold fast. We're turning."

They were less than half a mile from the shore when they turned and in less than five fathoms of water, and the waves were not as innocuous as they looked. As they swung broadside on, they rolled once again to within a hairsbreadth of turning turtle. Larsen needed all his strength and skill to haul them round into wind. Nor, when they had completed the turn, were their troubles over. For labouring straight into wind and sea, they made little progress—indeed if they moved at all, it seemed they were still being bludgeoned backward into the ice.

Again the warning throbbed through Larsen's brain: "Cut the tow; you'll make no headway until you cut the tow." But having dragged the blue so far, he wasn't, he told himself, going to lose it now. He rang for full power, and their turbines increased in revolution till the deck vibrated under his feet like a scenic railway. Even then it was several minutes before *Petrel* began, painfully slowly, to draw away from the shoals.

* * *

They were transferring Johan from stretcher to bunk when the warning came over the tannoy that *Petrel* was altering course. There was no time to secure him before the ship swung beam onto sea. The deck heeled over. One of the whalers lost his footing and slid, dragging the stretcher with him, the width of the saloon, and the others grabbed Johan and pressed him against the side of the bunk. They held him pressed tight to the bunk while the deck cartwheeled this way and that like an animal in convulsion; not till their bow came round into wind and they were again riding comparatively easily did they dare to release him.

It does a man with a broken leg no good to hold him pinned to a bulkhead.

They pulled off his sodden oilskins and boots, cut away his trousers, and took a closer look at his leg. None of them had a great deal of medical knowledge, but they had enough sense to realize that the less they touched a compound fracture the better. Torstein wiped the sweat off the old whaler's face. "Don't move, and we'll bed you down so as you're warm and still. You hurt anywhere except your leg?"

"No. Is the bracelet holding?"

"The bracelet's fine."

"You sure?"

"Carl, go on deck and check. And, deckie"—the boy was hovering anxiously in the companionway—"nip aft and brew us some tea."

They made Johan as comfortable as they could, using

pillows and blankets to wedge him in firmly; then they raised the height of the fiddles (to prevent his rolling out) and swabbed down his leg with antiseptic. The leg wasn't a pretty sight. The tibia had not fractured cleanly but had splintered into two serrated fangs which perforated the skin about four inches below the knee, while the fibula was not only broken but crushed; there had been a good deal of bleeding at first, but now that the leg was raised and still this had stopped. He lay motionless and without complaint, but they could tell by the sweat on his face that he was in considerable pain. It was a welcome diversion when Carl came back with news of the bracelet—the chief engineer, he told them, had hauled it tight, and the blue was once more firmly in tow —and another diversion when the boy brought in the tea. Torstein poured, dropping into Johan's mug four cubes of sugar and four aspirin. He then told the boy to open the spirit locker and bring back a bottle of rum. He was none too happy about offering Johan alcohol— indeed, he had a vague recollection of having been told that in cases of brain injury or hemorrhage it was dangerous—but he knew on the other hand that nothing saps an injured man's strength more surely than prolonged and continuous pain.

"Take a swig, Johan."

"You reckon it's okay to?"

"Sure. Drown your sorrows."

He drank about a sixth of the bottle.

One by one the whalers drifted away, not wanting

to leave, but knowing there was work on deck and that they could do no good by staying. Soon the saloon was empty except for Johan, Torstein and the deckie.

"Let me stay with him. Please!" The boy pulled up a chair to the side of the bunk.

Torstein nodded. With more than enough to cope with on deck, he was glad of the offer. "Right. I'll send someone to relieve you in a couple of hours." As he opened the door he turned; he was about to add, "And mind you, don't fall asleep," but when he saw the way that the boy was looking at Johan he went out with the warning unsaid.

* * *

"Scheer up, lad." The boy wasn't sure if the voice from the bunk was slurred with pain or with rum. "Plenty o' men ha' bust a leg one year an' been back whalin' the next."

"I know." He bathed the sweat from the old man's forehead. "Anything you'd like me to do?"

"Just talk. Or maybe read."

"Shall I read you one of your Westerns?"

As *Petrel's* bow dipped into a milestone, Johan screwed up his eyes; then, not trusting himself to unclench his teeth, he nodded. The boy went to the door of the saloon and shouted till one of the crew came slithering over. He explained what he wanted, then sat down again beside the bunk. "Nils is bringing a book."

Johan nodded. He was glad of the boy's company, but it embarrassed him that he was unable to hide his pain.

As if sensing his thoughts, the boy reached for the bottle
of rum. "You fancy a drop more?"

"Might as well." He drank rather more than a sixth this
time. Then Nils came in with the book.

Johan and his Westerns were something of a joke
aboard *Petrel*. His cabin was full of them—hardbacks,
paperbacks, pulps and magazine serials; classics like Hay-
cox and Zane Grey, and moderns like Luke Short, Will
Cook and Hendryx; he never read anything else. "What
has he brought?"

"*The Light of the Western Stars.*"

"Ah, the master!"

"You want me to start at the beginning?"

"Rather you start at the cattle muster. If I remember
right, that's round about chapter five."

As the boy found the place and began to read, the
old whaler closed his eyes, letting the words flow over
him like the warmth from a comforting fire. "*The great
mass of cattle,*" John Larsen read, "*seemed to be eddying
like a whirlpool. But when Madeline looked at one end
of the herd she saw cows standing still, facing outward,
and calves cringing close in fear. The motion of the
cattle slowed from the inside of the herd to the outside
and gradually ceased. The roar and tramp of hoofs and
crack of horns and thump of heads also ceased in degree,
but the bawling and bellowing continued. While she
watched, the herd spread, grew less dense, and stragglers
appeared to be about to bolt through the line of mounted
cowboys.*

"From that moment so many things happened, and so swiftly, that Madeline could not see a tenth of what was going on within eyesight. It seemed horsemen darted into the herd and drove out cattle. Madeline pinned her gaze on one cowboy who rode a white horse and was chasing a steer. He whirled a lasso around his head and threw it; the rope streaked out and the loop caught the leg of the steer. The white horse stopped with wonderful suddenness, and the steer slid in the dust. Quick as a flash the cowboy was out of the saddle, and, grasping the legs of the steer before it could rise, he tied them with a rope . . ." He glanced at Johan. The old whaler's eyes were glazed with pain, but he was smiling, lost in another world to the ice-cold seas of the south.

The boy read on, *"The lithe, dark vaqueros fascinated her. They were here, there, everywhere, with lariats flying, horses plunging back, jerking calves and yearlings to the grass. . . . They were swift, graceful, daring; they never failed to catch a running steer, and their lassos always went true. What sharp dashes the horses made, and wheelings here and there, and sudden stops, and how they braced themselves to withstand the shock!*

"The cowboys, likewise, showed wonderful horsemanship, and, reckless as they were, Madeline imagined she saw consideration for steed and cattle that was wanting in the vaqueros. They changed mounts oftener than the Mexican riders, and the horses they unsaddled for fresh ones were not so spent, so wet, so covered with

lather. *It was only after an hour or more of observation that Madeline began to realize the exceedingly toilsome and dangerous work cowboys had to perform. There was little or no rest for them. They were continually among wild and vicious and wide-horned steers. In many instances they owed their lives to their horses. The danger came mostly when the cowboy leaped off to tie and brand a calf he had thrown. Some of the cows charged with lowered, twisting horns. Time and again Madeline's heart leaped to her throat for fear a man would be gored. . . ."*

He glanced again at Johan. His eyes were closed now, and he looked to be fast asleep. But to be sure the boy read on to the end of the page. *"All the while this ceaseless activity was going on there was a strange uproar— bawl and bellow, the shock of heavy bodies meeting and falling, the shrill jabbering of the vaqueros, and the shouts and banterings of the cowboys. They took sharp orders and replied in jest. They went about this stern toil as if it were a game to be played in good humour. One sang a rollicking song, another whistled, another smoked a cigarette. The sun was hot, and they, like their horses, were dripping with sweat. . . ."*

He closed the book softly, keeping his place with a finger. The old whaler's eyes flickered open. "Ah, they were men, them cowboys. You'll not find the likes o' them today."

"I thought you were asleep, Johan. You like me to go on?"

"Think of it, lad. The sun, the steers and the great big silent deserts. How'd you have liked a life like that?"

"Sounds a bit cruel and hard."

"The country, not the men."

The boy was silent.

"You mustn't confuse them, lad. Maybe that's bin your mistake."

He said nothing.

"Tell me"—the old whaler raised himself on his elbow—"what is it you haven't liked aboard *Petrel*?"

"Let it ride, Johan."

"Runnin' away from a problem won't never solve it."

The boy would have liked to withdraw into his shell, to seek refuge as in times of difficulty he had sought refuge so often before in the make-believe world of his dreams, but he knew that Johan wanted to help. What should he tell him? Most of the things that he disliked about whaling were matters of atmosphere rather than fact; he cast around for something concrete onto which he could pin his dislike. "Don't much care," he said at last, "for seeing the whales killed."

"We none of us care for that."

"But you come back and watch, Johan. Year after year."

"Killin' ain't the be all and end all o' whaling."

"It is for the whale."

Old Johan shook his head. "Not really. Sometimes things have to die, you know, before they can live."

"Oh, Johan! Isn't that just so many words?"

"Reckon not. How d'you suppose our Lord Jesus Christ could have saved us all by His resurrection if He hadn't been crucified first?"

The boy scratched his ear. "Don't rightly know." A little embarrassed at the turn the conversation had taken, he thumbed through *The Light of the Western Stars.* "You like me to go on reading?"

"Not for a while. Now be honest, lad. What is it that's *really* bin eatin' you?"

For a long time the boy was silent, then he said slowly, "It's hard to explain, Johan. But I don't really feel I'm one of the crew. Even now. It's as if the rest of you are a team and I'm sort of left out."

"Like when you're not given rum in your tea?"

Their eyes met. "Silly, isn't it? When I don't even like the stuff!"

Johan eased himself up on his bunk. "As I told you before, lad, you're too impatient. You got to walk before you can run. You got to serve an apprenticeship before you become a whaler. Now wait." He held up a hand as the boy was about to interrupt. "I know what you're goin' to say—that you don't know how long your apprenticeship'll last, that there ain't no sort o' test you can take to end it. Well, that's the way it is with whalin'. Some lads come south year after year; somehow they don't measure up, so they're not accepted an' they drift away. Others fit in their very first season."

"And how'll I know when I've 'measured up'? Or if I'm ever going to?"

"The feelin' may come gradual; it may come all of a sudden, overnight. But when it does come it'll come for sure. An' you'll know."

The tannoy clicked to transmit. There was a crackle of atmospherics, then Larsen's voice blared into the saloon: "It took us nearly a couple of hours to fix the bracelet and get back on course. So we're behind schedule. We've got to cover thirty-two miles now in twenty-two hours. If we average a couple of knots, we'll do it easy. If we average a knot and a half—which is what we're making now—we'll squeeze in by the skin of our teeth, round about eleven-thirty tonight. We're clear of the shoals and pretty soon we'll be turning onto our final leg. This'll put us beam into sea. Beam into sea, we'll roll our guts out. And I want no accidents."

As the tannoy clicked dead, the boy looked at Johan. "I'll wedge you in," he said, "as tight as I can." He checked the fiddles for security, rearranged the pillows to counteract roll rather than pitch, and offered Johan the bottle of rum.

The old whaler shook his head. "Not till I have to."

"You like me to read?"

He nodded.

The boy had barely found his place when *Petrel* swung onto her new heading: 085° magnetic; beam on to the fifty-foot seas.

She began to roll then, with a sickening, corkscrewing sogginess that was accentuated by the dead weight of the carcass lashed to her beam. And she went on rolling, endlessly, without a second of respite, crabbing up the mountainous slopes, trembling for a moment on the wind-lashed summits, then toppling out of control into the maw, of the following troughs. Her deck was flung this way and that at the most violent and unpredictable angle, her engines now idled, now raced, and her plates ground out a continuous cacophony of complaint. And after a while the boy became aware of another sound, over and above the roar of the storm and the thousand and one little sounds of the ship. It was some moments before he realized what it was: the grinding of Johan's teeth.

Tears pricked at the back of his eyes. He moved to the bunk and held the old man's hand very tightly. It was his inability to help that distressed him most, his impotence in the face of suffering. "Isn't there *anything* I can do, Johan?"

"Pass me the rum. An' maybe go on readin'."

He held the bottle to the old man's lips, rearranged the pillows, and found his place in *The Light of the Western Stars*. He couldn't see the point himself in reading of cowboys and Indians, but it seemed to make Johan happy . . .

"*Then Stilwell,*" he read, "*began to talk. 'Miss Majesty, you're seein' the life of the cattlemen an' cowhands same as it was in the early days . . . Long hours on horseback, poor grub, sleepin' on the ground, lonesome watches, dust an' sun an' wind an' thirst, day in an' day out all the year round—that's what a cowboy has.*

" 'Look at Nels there. See, what little hair he has is snowwhite. He's red an' thin an' hard—burned up. You notice that hump on his shoulders. An' his hands, when he gets close—just take a peep at his hands. Nels can't pick up a pin. He can't hardly button his shirt or untie a knot in his rope. He looks sixty years—an old man. Wal, Nels ain't seen forty. He's a young man, but he's seen a lifetime for every year. It was Arizona that made Nels what he is, the Arizona desert an' the work of cowman. He's been ridin' at Cañon Diablo an' the Verde an' Tonto Basin. He knows every mile of Aravaipa Valley an' the Pinalena country. He's ranged from Tombstone to Douglas. He hed shot bad white men an' bad Greasers before he was twenty-one. He's seen some life, Nels has. My sixty years ain't nothin'; my early days in the Staked Plains an' on the border with Apaches ain't nothin' to what Nels has seen an' lived through. He's just come to be part of the desert; you might say he's stone an' fire an' silence an' cactus an' force. He's a man, Miss Majesty, a wonderful man. Rough he'll seem to you. Wal, I'll show you pieces of quartz from the mountains back of my ranch an' they're that rough they'd cut your hands. But there's pure gold in them. An' so it is with Nels an' many of these cowboys.' "

He glanced at Johan. He was breathing less quickly and his face had lost the worst of its pallor. "Ah, they was men, them cowboys. The last o' the frontiersmen."

The boy considered this. And it came to him quite suddenly why Johan got so much pleasure out of reading his Westerns. He and Zane Grey's heroes were two of a kind. "Don't know about that," he said slowly. "Aren't whalers frontiersmen too?"

The old man nodded, but without enthusiasm—he was in too much pain to assimilate ideas.

The boy realized that listening was easier for Johan than talking, so he went on reading, looking up every now and then in the hope of finding he had dozed off. For a long time sleep was denied to Johan, but he did in time drift into a coma, a state of semiconsciousness in which the pain of his leg was never absent but was softened and made more bearable by the haze of alcohol and dreams.

And while the boy read and the old man dozed, *Petrel* fought for her life in the heart of the storm.

The storm was a miscreation. It had built up too quickly to conform to the usual Antarctic pattern, also it was travelling too fast, and the winds at its perimeter were fiercer than those at its core. It had, in fact, many of the characteristics of a Caribbean hurricane—hence the temporary easing off of wind and sea as *Petrel* passed through its center. The waves were still enormous here, dropping only from fifty feet to round about forty, but the wind was considerably less and there was no snow.

In the improved conditions Johan, after a while, was able to lie in something approaching comfort, lulled to a sense of false relief by the thought that the worst of the storm was over. What neither he nor anyone else realized was that the worse was still to come, that in the cold front swinging down in the wake of the depression, winds and seas were even more frenetic than those they had already fought through.

By 3 A.M. Larsen was so confident that the weather had taken a turn for the better that he left the bridge and made his way to the saloon. He was surprised to find his son still sitting with Johan, reading. As he tip-toed to the bunk, the boy raised a finger to his lips. "Is he," Larsen whispered, "asleep?"

"No. Just dozing."

Larsen noticed the white of his son's face and the dark circles under his eyes. "You've been with Johan a long time. Reckon you're due for a turn below."

"You've been on the bridge even longer, Dad. Are *you* going below?"

Larsen scratched his ear. "Reckon we could both do with a change. How'd it be if I stayed with Johan while you have a nap?"

The boy hesitated. He was nearly asleep on his feet, but so, he knew, was his father, and if his father could carry on, so could he. "Johan likes me to read to him."

"I'll read"—Larsen picked up *The Light of the Western Stars*—"and if he asks for you, I'll give you a call."

"Promise?"

"Cross my heart."

As they stood for a moment beside the bunk the old whaler moved restlessly, muttering, his face creased with pain.

"Dad!" The boy's voice was anxious. "They'll not amputate his leg, will they?"

"Not as long as we keep him still."

It was as though a great weight had been lifted from the boy's mind. "I'd never forgive myself," he said, "if he lost his leg." And he ran quickly out of the saloon.

He wanted, before dossing down, to have a look at the weather. The moment he set foot on deck he was conscious of its improvement. The snow had stopped, and the wind had lost the edge of its malevolence; it was roaring now rather than shrieking, and it no longer ripped up whole patches of sea and flung them from crest to crest. He hung on to a life line, smiling. The worst, he thought, was over; they were going to make it; everything was coming right. He walked across to the barometer. He expected to find it risen, but it was still at its nadir: 28.2. Indeed, when he tapped it, the needle dropped still farther. Puzzled, he was about to tap it again when he noticed the smell of blood.

There was only one place such a smell could come from. He worked his way to the port quarter and stared at the blue. What he saw was not exactly a surprise, but even so, the grotesquely inflated tongue, streaming blood, made his face crease up in distaste. It was not unusual, he knew, for the tongue of a dead whale to inflate and bleed, for when a whale carcass is towed through heavy seas salt water is forced down its throat and this, mingling with the compressed air in its stomach, sets up a chemical action which causes the membrane of the tongue to swell up like a balloon; the tongue then spills out of the whale's mouth, is battered by the waves, and begins to bleed. The boy had seen it often enough in the last few months. He was about to turn away, disinterested, when he saw something else: the black triangular fin.

It cut through the arc light, fast as a torpedo and heading straight for the blue. Was it imagination or did the carcass, the ship and the boy quiver together as thirty razor-sharp teeth slashed into the body of the whale, ripping off in a single bite ten pounds of blubber?

John Larsen's face turned white, and sweat broke out in little beads on his forehead. For he knew that in all the sea lanes of Antarctica there is only one creature with a black triangular fin, *Orcinus orcae*, the killer whale. He knew, too, that killer whales hunt in packs, that they attack anything edible on sight, and that in less than ten minutes they can reduce a full-grown whale to a worthless cavity of bone.

Again the carcass quivered; and the sea in their wake turned red.

* * *

Larsen was rearranging old Johan's pillows when the door burst open.

"Killers!"

For the first time since taking the blue in tow, he was afraid. He had noticed some hours ago that its tongue was bleeding, but he had reckoned the weather too bad for a pack of killers to pick up the scent. He had, it seemed, been wrong. He half slithered, half fell down the hatch, knowing every second was vital. The rifles and ammunition were locked in a cupboard under his bunk.

As he pulled them out, Bengt Nielsen came clattering down the companionway. "One for me, Svend? Please."

He heistated. They carried only two rifles—short Lee Enfields. Torstein would want one and he had been going to use the other; but Bengt was their crack marksman. He tossed him a rifle and two clips of .303. "Watch out for ricochets."

On deck a group of whalers, the boy among them, were leaning over the guardrail, staring in appalled fascination at the killers. There seemed to be only the pair of them for the moment, two black triangular fins astab at the body of the blue; but others, Larsen knew, would be with them before long. Anger engulfed him. To have risked so much and to have towed their prize so far, only to lose it to a pack of benighted dolphins!*

The same sort of exasperation had taken hold of Bengt Nielsen; and he, being more impulsive and less experienced than Larsen, attempted a shot the second he set foot on deck. As he came tumbling out of the companionway, *Petrel* was climbing a wave on whose crest killers and carcass were raised to eye level as if on a stage, and one of the killers, mouth agape, was heading straight for the blue—the sort of target, it seemed to Bengt, that he might never be offered again. Instinctively

---

* *Orcinus Orcae* (generally known as killer whales or grampuses) are in fact misnamed members of the dolphin family. Twenty-five feet in length, twenty-five tons in weight, black-backed and yellow-bellied, they are the most terrifying and ferocious creatures on earth.

J.V.M.

his rifle swung up, and his finger tightened. But he had forgotten how steeply *Petrel* was rolling. In the same second that his bullet smacked into the killer his feet slid from under him. His hand, as he fell, clamped tight on the Lee Enfield; whatever happens, he thought, I mustn't let go. But he hit the deck awkwardly, elbow first; his arm went numb and his muscles limp, and the rifle slid out of his grasp and into the gunwhale. A whaler tried to grab it, but he, too, lost his footing and fell. When *Petrel* rolled back onto an even keel, the men picked themselves up, but the rifle had gone.

It had gone, but its bullet had not been fired in vain.

Hit between the eyes, the killer leapt from the water, flailed briefly, then floated out of the arc light, streaming blood. It is one of the less attractive traits of *Orcinus orcae* that if a member of the pack is injured, the others eat it alive. The killer was still twitching when its companion's teeth ripped open its belly. For a couple of minutes, as the great creatures threshed and flailed in *Petrel's* wake, the carcass was undisturbed. But Larsen knew that the rest of the pack would soon be drawn toward them by the smell of blood as iron is drawn to a magnet. And they had only the one rifle to keep them at bay.

A whaler turned to the boy. "You'd best go below, lad."

"No. Please!"

"Johan'd be glad of your company."

He shook his head. He knew what the whaler was

thinking—that some things it is better not to see—but he just couldn't accept that the whale which meant so much to him was about to be ripped to pieces in front of his eyes. We've beaten the clock, he thought, and the storm and the shoals and the parted tow; surely we'll beat the killers too!

At least, it seemed, they were going to try. For as he stood by the rail, trying desperately to think of how they could keep the *Orcinus orcae* at bay, a group of whalers came clattering onto the foredeck. They pulled open the door of the rope locker and dragged out a bundle of markers. Working quickly, they wrapped the markers in paraffin-soaked rags and lashed them to the rail. Then they set them ablaze—fire to deter and light to shoot by. And for a while the light of the flares and the bullets of the Lee Enfield kept the killers at a distance.

But as their numbers increased, the *Orcinus orcae* grew bolder. They came in singly at first, hovering beyond the flare light, then darting one at a time at the carcass. But as the blue began to bleed more freely, they closed in, worrying at it continuously like wolves at an injured bear. Soon there were fifteen to twenty of them tearing at the carcass. Each time their teeth ripped into it, it quivered, and the boy quivered too—it was his dreams that the razor-edged teeth were tearing to shreds.

From the bridge Larsen kept up a continuous but largely ineffective fire, ineffective because *Petrel* was rolling heavily, the killers moved fast, and only a shot in head or heart had noticeable effect. He was fighting a

losing battle. And he knew it. Torstein suggested they
fire the Vereys—two-star distress rockets—and to this
he agreed, though without much hope of success. Out of
the corner of his eye he watched the mate as he collected
pistol and cartridges, watched him take careful aim,
and watched the two-star-red detonate with a muffled
thud in the sea. The result was anticlimax. The killers
took not the slightest notice. But Torstein didn't give up.
He went on firing. And eventually one of his shots lodged
in a killer's back. At first the great creature appeared
to be unaffected, but the blood seeping out of his shoulder was his death warrant; even as he tore at the blue his
fellows were on him, their teeth slashing open the wound
in his shoulder. He fought for his life fiercely but briefly,
and soon no trace of his body remained, and the pack
were atug once more at the carcass of the whale. If only,
Larsen thought, we could wound three or four of them
at the same time.

The same thought had occurred to his son. He had
plenty of ideas, but most of them were more ingenious
than practicable—jettisoning oil to seal up the killers'
lungs (but the storm would disperse it too quickly),
spraying the killers with a high-pressure hose (but the
wind would deaden the force of its jet), firing the Svend
Foyn (but they couldn't bring it to bear so close under
their quarter) . . . and yet surely, he thought, they could
make *some* use of the gun and its 180-pound harpoons.
It came to him suddenly, a flash of inspiration, and he
was scrambling onto the bridge. "Dad! Dad! I know
how we can stop 'em!"

"How?"

"Hand grenades."

"But we haven't any!"

"We can make them. With the fuse of a harpoon and gunpowder."

A sudden coldness seeped into every part of Larsen's body, the coldness of fear. For he saw that grenades *could* be the answer, but that they could, on the other hand, kill not only the *Orcinus orcae* but also the better part of his crew. Improvising with detonators and gunpowder, he told himself, was a fool's game at the best of times; in a force-ten hurricane with the ship rolling gunwhale under it would be suicide. He was about to shake his head when Torstein said quietly, "I'll make them."

Don't risk it, the familiar drumbeat throbbed through his brain; don't risk your crew for the sake of your son. And yet Torstein, he knew, was not the man to gamble his life lightly, so the risk, to him, must appear to be not too great. He passed a hand over his eyes, and the tiredness and strain of the last forty-eight hours swept over him like the maw of a giant wave. "No," he heard himself say, "it's not worth it."

He felt the mate's hand on his shoulder. "You and I could do it, Svend. Together."

No other argument would have moved him. But a challenge—and a personal challenge at that—was something he couldn't resist. This was his strength and his weakness—that he was never willing to admit defeat. With an almost physical effort he pushed his tiredness aside.

"Bengt"—he handed the whaler his rifle—"lose this, and you'll go overboard too! Helmsman, man the emergency steering aft! Jamie, clear the foredeck and bridge!"

As the crew took cover aft, Svend and Torstein got together the things that were needed: cordite cases from the storage bins, fifteen-pound grenades from the harpoon war heads, and powder from the between-decks storage. It was the same story as with resecuring the tow: two things were essential, speed and care. Speed, because the teeth of the killers, every second, were ripping away great ribbons of flesh—another five or ten minutes and the carcass would be too badly damaged for the factory ship to accept—and care because a mistake in assembling the grenades or a jolt at the critical moment and they would be blasted off the face of the earth.

They wedged themselves into a corner of the chartroom.

"How do we seal the cases?"

Larsen pushed over a pair of cork floats. "Cut these to size."

They worked in silence, pressing the open end of a spent container onto the float, making an impression, then cutting the cork into a plug that would eventually be wedged into the container's base. Next they each filled their container about two-thirds full of gunpowder. This was easy, for the gunpowder, which was used as a charge for the Svend Foyn, was kept in fourteen-pound bags with special funnel-shaped tops for easy pouring.

But then came the moment of danger. They each took
the priming device from a harpoon war head, defused
it, and carefully eased out the detonator. The detonators
—fulminate of mercury—were as sensitive to movement
as the skin of a chameleon to light. As he wormed the
thin glass rod into the gunpowder Larsen could feel
the sweat trickling out of his eyes. A sudden and quite
irrational fear took hold of him: that the sweat from
his eyes would fall onto the detonator like stone onto
glass. He could feel the beads, heavy and salt, gathering
on his eyelids; he didn't dare blink for fear of dislodging
them. For perhaps ten seconds he was too terrified to
move or think; then, with great concentration, he began
to pack more powder around the rod of the detonator.
A mistake here would cost them their lives. If the powder
were packed in too loosely, the detonator would shift,
knock against the side of the container, and be triggered
off; too tightly, and the pressure of kneading fingers
would break the glass. The ship rolled steeply, threatening to fling him against stanchion or bulkhead, sweat
ran into his eyes, his hands trembled, and the mouth of
the bag was too large to pour accurately into the container; gunpowder seeped grey onto the deck.

"I'm sealing mine." Torstein's voice came as if from
a long way away.

"Good!" He eased a few more grains into the container, pressed down on them with the tips of his fingers,
then reached for the improvised plug. It fitted well; in
fact it fitted exactly except for one tiny segment where

its perimeter was slightly serrated so that a gap of about an eighth of an inch was left between cork and container. He could see what would happen if the gap wasn't closed: powder would trickle out and the rod would work free and detonate. But to seal it would not be easy, and to cut another plug would take time.

He was faced with the all too familiar problem: should he take a risk? Should he throw the grenade while it was still not properly sealed?

In the few seconds that it took him to reach a decision, the events of the last twenty-four hours passed through his mind with the clarity of a nightmare. And he saw, quite clearly, that he had taken too many risks already. It had started with the haloed moon—when he had seen it he ought to have run for shelter; when he had heard that the buoy boats were stormbound he ought to have abandoned the whale; when *Petrel* had almost turned turtle he ought to have cut the tow; when one bracelet had parted he ought to have slipped the other; when they had run into shoal water he ought to have reversed course, and when his son had suggested homemade grenades he ought to have shaken his head. He had gambled time after time. And won. His luck couldn't hold forever. And yet again, a voice whispered, having risked so much, are you now going to throw it all away for fear of taking the one last chance? His hands clenched tight on the case of the grenade. His head warned him that another risk would be one too many, but his heart implored him to make this one last throw for the sake of his son.

"Ready, Svend?" The mate was looking at him curiously.

He nodded. "We'll throw together. We'll go to the rail. I'll say, 'One, two, three, throw,' and the jerk of the throw will break the detonators."

"I'm ready."

They got to their feet. Carefully. A stumble, a slip, or a sudden move and they would have three seconds to live. As they edged out of the chartroom, the chief engineer motioned the crew under cover, and a line of heads ducked under the engine-room casing.

As they reached the rail the killers were wrenching en masse at the blue—eighteen to twenty of them, circling the carcass in a gluttonous *danse macabre*.

"Aim for the middle of 'em."

Torstein nodded.

For perhaps half a minute they stood by the rail, getting the feel of *Petrel's* movement, waiting for her to sway onto a more or less even keel. Then Larsen's fingers tightened. "One, two, three, throw!"

Their arms swung back. And the grenades sailed spinning into the night.

They burst almost simultaneously, one ten feet up and the other flush on the water. And the result was a holocaust. A few fragments of shrapnel sliced into *Petrel's* hull, and a few more sank harmlessly into the sea; the rest tore into the *Orcinus orcae*.

About a third of them were killed instantly and another third injured. Any other creatures, struck by so savage a blast of destruction, would have turned and fled; but the killers, in blood lust, turned on each other. The living flung themselves on the dead, their teeth ripping open the bodies of their companions with the same bestial greed as they had ripped into the body of the blue. Even the hardened whalers who had rushed to the rail turned away in nausea. They loathed the killers with a deep-rooted aversion that they felt for no other creature, but they would not have wished even a killer a death such as this.

As *Petrel* ploughed on into the storm, the patch of incarnadined sea dropped slowly astern, drifting first out of the glow of their flares, then out of the circle of arch light, and finally out of the white of their wake. But for several minutes, even above the roar of wind and sea, the thud of great bodies came juddering out of the dark.

After a while a couple of killers tried to nose back, but they were driven off by the combined fire of the Lee Enfield and Vereys. Within five minutes of the grenades being thrown the carcass had ceased to quiver. And within ten minutes the world had reverted once more to its two components—the ship and the storm.

Leaning over the rail, the whalers peered anxiously at the blue. It was streaming blood; dark caverns pitted its sides, and ribbons of flesh trailed like spilled entrails out of its belly. But it was still, quite definitely, a carcass fit to be processed; it was still their two hundredth whale.

The boy was beside himself with elation.

"Good idea of yours, deckie!" The mate's hand was on his shoulder.

"Was it very difficult, Torstein? To make the grenades?"

"More tricky than difficult. Now you and I had better be making tea."

Surprised, he looked at his watch. It was 4 A.M.—only half an hour till dawn and the ritual of hot tea and rum.

They made their way to the galley, switched on the ovens, and filled the pans; then, while Torstein unlocked the spirit locker, the boy set about washing and drying a dozen mugs. The rolling, it seemed to him, was far more noticeable in the galley. Twice he was flung from sink to bulkhead as *Petrel* fell awkwardly into a trough. He thought at first that it must be the confined space which appeared to accentuate the movement of the ship, but when he suggested this to Torstein the mate shook his head. "The rolling *is* worse."

"I thought the weather was getting better."

"So did I. But it looks as if we were wrong."

He didn't like the sound of that. He had hoped that, having disposed of the killers, the rest of the tow would be plain sailing; but if wind and sea again took a turn for the worse, their troubles were obviously far from over.

"Dry the mugs properly, lad."

The boy sighed. He wished that now he had done his share—and more—in clearing the ice and driving away the killers, the rest of the crew would stop calling him "deckie" or "lad" and would use his Christian name, the same as they did with each other. But it was not, it seemed, to be. He had harboured a secret hope, too, that when the time came they would offer him rum in his tea, as a token they at last recognized him as a whaler. But here again he was disappointed. His mug, at four-thirty, was pushed across to him without the tot that was measured so carefully into the others'. He had no intention of letting them see how he felt. He simply asked for another mug for Johan and said he was going aft.

He was obliged to make two journeys to the saloon—one with his mug, one with Johan's—and even then he lost most of the tea enroute. For *Petrel* once again was rolling steeply and viciously, corkscrewing gunwhale under among waves of a full fifty feet.

He was pleased to find Johan awake; he had been looking forward to telling him how it was *his* idea that he saved the whale. But as he drew up his chair to the bunk, his pleasure drained quickly away. For Johan's face was grey and beaded with sweat, and he looked ill enough to be dying.

* * *

There is no need to be afraid, the boy told himself; he has only broken a leg, and you can't die of a broken leg. He sat down, intending to recount his prowess in driving away the *Orcinus orcae*, but the pain in the old man's eyes made his achievement seem suddenly hollow.

"Can I fix your pillows, Johan?"

The old whaler nodded. A couple of hours ago he had been dozing in comparative comfort; but *Petrel* was rolling more wickedly now than ever before, and he was being flung from side to side of his bunk. And he would, the boy realized, go on being flung from side to side of his bunk so long as the storm continued and *Petrel* stayed beam into sea—and the storm now looked as though it might continue for days, and they would be beam into sea the whole way back to *Cyclopean*, i.e., for at least another fourteen to sixteen hours.

The boy packed pillows and wads of cotton wool round the old man's leg as tightly as he could, but even as he was arranging them they began to work loose under the violent movement of the ship. And there was nothing he could do about it, nothing he could do to help as the deck was flung this way and that, steeply and unpredictably, now heeling over in a low slow slide to port, now hesitating, gunwhale under, as though *Petrel* was wondering whether to right herself or sink, exhausted, to oblivion, and then coming back with gathering momentum in an uncontrollable sweep to starboard. *Petrel* suffered that morning as in the cold front following the depression wind and sea built up to a second and still more tumultuous climax; but her suffering was nothing to that of Johan.

He lay on his back one hand grasping the fiddles and the other the bulkhead in an effort to stop himself being flung to the deck. His broken leg was never still but was subjected to a thousand and one little pressures and

movements, the bones now grating together, now pressing onto a nerve, now pushing a shade more acutely
through the shattered membrane of his kneecap. Before
long, blood began to seep through the sheets; his breathing quickened, and his face took on a greyness that the
boy didn't like.

"More rum, Johan?"

He had drunk three-quarters of the bottle already.
But he reached for it eagerly, drained it as an addict his
opiate, and in a few minutes was moistening his lips for
more. He was in too much pain to be granted the oblivion
of the drunk, but the alcohol did do a little to deaden
the worst of his agony.

The boy stayed close to him, bathing the sweat out
of his eyes, holding his hand, rearranging his pillows,
sometimes talking and sometimes reading from *The Light
of Western Stars*. At first their conversation was rea-
sonably coherent, but as the hours passed, the old whaler's
speech became increasingly slurred and his mind increasingly confused. By midmorning he was walking the
world of his dreams, the sun-dried deserts of Arizona.

How serious, the boy wondered, was delirium? He
kept hold of Johan's hand, trying to follow the thread
of the old man's thoughts as he muttered of cattle mus-
ters, floods and the Apache. Most of the time he seemed
unconscious of his surroundings, but every now and
then he would come to and talk quite rationally. It was
in one such moment that he noticed the boy's eyes were
full of tears.

"Don't fret, lad. There's worse troubles in the desert!"

"Oh, Johan! I'd give *anything* to help. If only we hadn't lost the morphine!"

"Forget it! Them cowboys hadn't no morphine . . ." And he drifted away once more into a world where the boy couldn't follow.

The hours passed. The storm grew fiercer and Johan weaker.

At the start of the second watch a whaler came into the saloon and suggested the boy went below. But he wouldn't leave. He had a tender heart and the sight of Johan's suffering distressed him almost beyond endurance; yet he stayed by his side hour after hour, not knowing how he could help, but sensing instinctively that the old whaler was glad of his presence. Time passed slowly that morning and the boy had plenty of opportunity to think; too much opportunity, in fact, for his peace of mind, for his thoughts after a while took a turn that was decidedly uncomfortable.

When he had come into the saloon with Johan's tea, he had been mighty pleased with himself, puffed up with satisfaction at the thought that it was *his* idea that had saved *his* whale. But after a while the pain in Johan's eyes made him begin to wonder if the fate of his whale was all that important compared to the fate of Johan's leg; and the more he thought about this the more his satisfaction gave way to an uneasy feeling of guilt. What was it, he asked himself, that he had said to his father? That he would never forgive himself if Johan lost his leg? Yet he could see that if *Petrel* stayed beam into sea for another fourteen or fifteen hours, then Johan's leg might well have to be amputated. But what, he asked himself, could *he* do about this? *He* wasn't *Petrel's* skipper. *He* couldn't turn the ship head into wind so that she rode more easily and Johan could sleep.

He sat by the old whaler's side, watching the wildly tilting bulkheads and listening to the cacophony of the storm. Several times he found that his eyes and his head were drooping, but he willed himself not to fall asleep. A lot of use I'd be to Johan, he thought, asleep! After a while he let go of the old man's hand and felt his pulse. He didn't know much about taking pulses, but he could tell that Johan's was far too faint and rapid.

A little after ten o'clock Bengt Nielsen came into the saloon. "Nip aft, lad, for your breakfast. I'll keep an eye on Johan."

"Can't I stay with him? Please?"

"Torstein's orders. If you don't eat, we'll have *you* on the sick list too!"

He didn't realize how hungry he was until he got to the galley and saw the food they had left for him—porridge, cocoa and thick slices of buttered bread. There had been no sit-down meal since the previous evening, the crew as they came off duty simply snatching what food they could, and he now had the galley to himself. He settled into a corner between air vents and ovens and sipped his cocoa.

He heard the voices at once. He couldn't for a moment

think where they came from; then the trembling of the air vent gave him a clue. A pair of whalers were dislodging ice outside the galley where they were sheltered from the worst of the storm. They were talking, and their voices were being swept into the air vents and magnified as if in an amplifier. If he listened carefully, he could hear everything they said.

Listeners, he told himself, hear no good of themselves; but on the other hand, the whalers were hardly likely to be talking of him. He listened. They were cursing the ice, which had solidified along the side of the galley into a tough adhesive ridge. The thud of their hammers and their grunts and imprecations came through quite clearly, together with the crash of waves and the pulsating roar of the wind. He had almost finished his porridge before he heard anything of interest; then, it seemed, a third whaler joined the pair at work on the ice.

"Ah, Carl! How is he?"

"Not too good." The boy recognized the voice of the younger Nielsen.

"Hmmm! Who's with him?"

"Bengt. The lad's gettin' a bite in the galley."

The boy told himself that he wasn't *really* eavesdropping, because he had no alternative but to listen—he couldn't very well bang on the air vent and shout, "Hey, I can hear you." Or could he? By the time he had made up his mind, he had heard too much.

"You reckon he'll lose his leg?" The voice, as if echoing the boy's fears, came suddenly out of the air vent.

"Reckon he might."

"Hmmm! Pity we got to stay beam into sea."

"That's puttin' it mildly!"

A pause, then: "You reckon Svend'll alter course."

"Not unless he's asked to . . . Hey, look at this!" The air vent vibrated to a series of blows from the hammers. "That's shifted it. Let's move on." The voices faded as the ice breakers worked their way for'd.

The boy sat perfectly still, hands and eyes screwed tight as if to shut out what he had heard. But it was no good. He had known for some time in his heart the truth which the whalers' conversation had finally driven home—that there were two clear-cut alternatives. Either *Petrel* stayed on course (beam into sea)—in which case they would reach *Cyclopean* in time to earn the bonus, but the price would be twelve hours' agony for Johan and the probability of his losing his leg; or else *Petrel* altered course (and headed into the sea)—in which case she would ride a great deal easier and Johan could sleep, but the price would be their failure to reach *Cyclopean* in time to earn the bonus and the end of his dreams of the Academy. It was a question of which was more important: his dreams or Johan's leg.

And another thing the whalers' conversation brought home. Up to now he had told himself that since he was only the deckie *Petrel's* course was not a matter for *him* to worry about. But he now saw the fallacy of this. The blue was his; it was for his sake that the crew were striving to tow it back, and if the struggle was to be given up, it must be at his instigation.

He saw quite clearly then what he ought to do, but it was some time before he could bring himself to do it. But at last, trying desperately to shut his mind to the consequence of what he was going to ask, he buttoned up his oilskins and sou'wester, opened the door of the galley, and hooked himself on to a life line.

As he clawed his way for'd to the bridge he realized that the weather had worsened a great deal since they had driven away the *Orcinus orcae*. The seas were enormous now, the wind was back to well over a hundred knots, and it was snowing hard and was bitterly cold—far colder than it had been at dawn. He found his father taking a turn at the wheel. "Dad!" He had to shout to make himself heard above the roar of the storm.

"Hello, lad! How's Johan?"

"He's in terrible pain. We've got to do something or he'll lose his leg."

"What *can* we do?"

"We can turn into wind."

Larsen shook his head. "If we turn into wind we'll not get to *Cyclopean* by midnight."

"I know."

Larsen was exhausted, mentally as well as physically —in the last thirty hours he had had neither sleep nor rest—and it was some moments before the significance of what his son was saying got through to him. Then, suddenly, the implication struck home. "You mean"— his voice was incredulous—"you'd give up the bonus? For Johan?"

The boy's hands tightened. "You haven't seen him.

He's delirious. Maybe he's dying. We can't just sit and watch!"

His father stared at him. "Reckon," he said slowly, "I'd best have a look at Johan myself."

"There's no need to look at him. Please. Just turn into wind."

He means it now, Larsen thought, but he'll regret it later. He laid a hand on his son's shoulder. "No need to rush our fences. . . . Thor"—he turned to the starboard lookout—"take over the wheel. And you, lad, take over from Thor."

The boy opened his mouth, thought better of it, and walked to the starboard rail. As his father worked his way aft to the saloon, he did his best to concentrate on scanning the sea. But it wasn't easy. Snow beat, stinging, into his eyes; he quickly lost all feeling in hands and feet, and Johan's face, beaded with sweat, kept rising ghostlike out of the waves. After a while he cupped his hands to the helmsman's ear. "Are we meant to be looking for anything special?"

"Ice."

He remembered then the coldness that he had felt on coming out of the galley and paid more attention to scanning his segment of sea; the possibility of a chain of bergs bearing down on them on the heels of the storm was not to be taken lightly. Snow plastered up his binoculars, cold ate into his feet, and time dragged. His father and Johan, it seemed, were finding a lot to say to each other.

After a while he noticed that the lookout to port was focussing his binoculars on the sea ahead. He did the same. The great waves came heaving into his view finder, enlarged but frustratingly blurred. He strained his eyes. There was whiteness ahead—that he was sure of—but was the whiteness spume, snow squall, or mist? Or was it something more solid—and more lethal? He had just made up his mind that it was mist when a warning blared over the tannoy:

"Loose ice! Twenty degrees to port! . . ." And a moment later: "Two floes, a quarter of a mile on the beam."

Ice to port, he knew, could well be an augury of ice to starboard. He was scanning his section of the horizon with extra care when his father came scrambling back to the bridge.

Larsen spotted the floes right away: two sharp-edged

blocks, not much bigger than ship's boats, disappearing into the gloom on their quarter. They at least were no danger. "Anything to starboard?"

"Don't think so, Dad. But the sea ahead looks sort of white."

Larsen spent several minutes studying the whiteness that lay like a layer of marsh gas across their bow. He too identified it as mist. But whereas the boy had seen the mist and failed to interpret it, his father was able to interpret it only too well. Mid-ocean patches of mist in a force-nine storm could be caused, Larsen knew, by only one thing: the comparatively warm air stream hitting a chain of icebergs—a chain maybe several miles in length and several hundred feet in height bearing down on them at a speed of anything up to a dozen knots. His lips tightened. "Forty degrees to port. John, a word in the chartroom."

Larsen's attention was divided, half on the boy and half on the water ahead where he expected any moment to see great cliffs of ice come looming out of the mist; he did, however, make an effort as they climbed into the warmth of the chartroom to concentrate on one thing at a time. He laid a hand on his son's shoulder. "I'm real glad you asked me to turn into wind. But I reckon Johan's not as bad as you think. No"—he held up his hand as the boy began to protest—"hear me out, then you can have your say. I know he's your friend. I know he's in pain. And I know he'd be far better off if we *were* into wind. But whalers are tough. He'll survive. There's not the

slightest risk, I promise you, of his dying. . . ." Even as
he spoke his attention wandered to the sea ahead, and he
was unprepared for the vehemence of the boy's reaction.

"But if he loses his leg, he'll never come whaling
again."

"I know, but—"

"Then for God's sake, Dad, turn into wind."

Larsen would have liked to talk things over with his
son, to be sure that he wasn't saying on impulse what
he would later regret, but there was no time . . . That,
it came to him suddenly, had been the trouble all season;
he had been so busy with his ship and his whalers that he
hadn't given enough of his time to the boy—but it was
too late now. Even as he hesitated, the voice of the lookout came over the tannoy: "Ice dead ahead!"

"I must go."

"Promise you'll turn into wind when we've passed
the ice."

"I promise to think about it."

"But, Dad—"

Larsen climbed onto the bridge. He focussed his binoculars on the line of smooth white bluffs now protruding
quite clearly out of the mist on their starboard bow. He
again altered course and rang for an increase in speed.
The discussion was closed.

Sadly—for there is nothing more wounding than to
have one's sacrifice brushed aside—the boy made his
way to the saloon.

He found Johan awake and struggling to sit up. Their

forty-degree alteration of course had made a great deal of difference to *Petrel's* movement, and the old whaler was already far more comfortable. "Why've we turned into wind?" His voice was puzzled.

"Ice."

"Hmmm!" Johan was too hazed with alcohol and pain to be sure of what was going on, but he could tell that the boy was upset. "What's the matter, lad?"

"Nothing."

The old man looked at him owlishly. After a while he picked up *The Light of Western Stars*. "Would you go on readin'?"

"Sure."

The boy found his place and began to read automatically and without expression. The words meant nothing, but after a while—as Johan had known would happen— the need to concentrate on the typeset page took his mind off his unhappiness. What he read of failed to move him—the dusty herds and the far horizons conjured up no dreams for him as they did for Johan—but it is hard to read aloud of one thing and brood over another.

And as the boy read and the old whaler enjoyed an all too brief respite from *Petrel's* rolling, they worked their way through the ice.

There were two chains of icebergs—the larger to starboard and the smaller to port—with a gap of something like half a mile in between. It would have been safer, Larsen knew, to bypass the chain altogether by standing even farther out to sea, but this would have taken *Petrel* far off course and have wasted time. They had little time to play with. So he headed straight for the gap.

The bergs came drifting toward them, fast. From far off they had looked almost ethereal: translucent sculptures of white, wreathed in mist and fringed by a gossamer veil. But as the range closed, the ethereal whiteness hardened into great cliffs of adamant, and the gossamer veil was metamorphosed into a hundred-and-fifty-foot cascade of spray. As they stood through the gap, the thunder and crash of millions of tons of seething water drowned both the throb of *Petrel's* engines and the roar of the storm, while random winds, cold and humid, slammed into them from every point of the compass. And the gap was less than half a mile wide. Suppose, Larsen thought, a shift in wind and sea brings the bergs together? Suppose they are joined underwater and the sea in between them is shoaling? Suppose our rudder jams on a patch of ice? But his fears were groundless. They squeezed through the gap with only a few small alterations of course and with little loss of time. Within half an hour of the ice being sighted it was disappearing astern, and the world had reverted once more to its two components: the ship and the storm.

Larsen was filled with a great sense of achievement. He felt like an athlete, leading the field, who clears the last of a line of hurdles. They had, he told himself, faced up to all that Antarctica could throw at them—storm and shoal, killers and ice—and had come through, against all the odds, to within sight of their goal. Only one last decision had to be made (and it a formality): whether to hold course for *Cyclopean* or turn, as his son had suggested, bow into sea.

He decided to hold course.

He reached his decision with less heart searching than would have been indulged in by any of his crew. For the tow of the blue, which had started as a labour of love, had by now become an obsession. They were, he told himself, less than twenty miles from the factory ship; they would reach her well before midnight. It would be mad to give up all they had fought for for the sake of a quixotic impulse.

But his decision brought him no peace of mind. He told himself over and over again that he was acting sensibly, that he was doing what was best for his son. But a voice kept whispering that if his crew had begged him to give up the tow he would have agreed; why then wasn't he doing for his son what he would have done for his crew? For a long time he paced the bridge, prey to a complexity of doubts. But in the end he salved his conscience with the thought that his son was only a boy and couldn't therefore be expected to know what was best.

So *Petrel* went reeling on, hour after hour, beam into sea.

And there was no letting up in the pain that Johan was racked by.

While *Petrel* had been standing offshore to avoid the ice, the old whaler had been in comparative comfort; but now they were again running beam onto the gargantuan waves, his moment of respite was passed. And as morning passed into afternoon and the deck continued to cant this way and that, neither drugs nor sedatives, nor alcohol nor dreams, nor all the boy's ministrations could blunt for a second the edge of the old man's agony. Nor was his agony a transient thing. It went on and on, with every shaft of pain increasing the chances of his losing his leg.

By 1 P.M. John Larsen had seen enough. It seemed to him altogether wrong—downright wicked, in fact—that his bonus should be considered of more importance than Johan's leg. He knew from the conversation he had overheard in the galley that some of the crew felt as he did; so it was up to him, he told himself, to act as his every instinct cried was right.

It was the hammer which gave him the idea: the ten-pound hammer lashed to the bulkhead as part of the fire-fighting equipment stowed behind the door of the saloon.

He didn't come to a decision quickly or on the spur of the moment, but eventually, after a long and painful struggle, as a snake sloughs off the skin that has become too small, he cast aside that afternoon the dreams of his childhood. He didn't stop to think of the enormity of what he was about to do—of what his father would think, of whether the crew would understand, of the consequences to himself. He only knew that the sooner he did it the sooner Johan would be able to sleep in peace. And that was what mattered most.

He waited till the old whaler had lapsed into one of his semi-comas, then he climbed into his oilskins. He unlashed the hammer, hid it under the folds of his trousers, and eased open the door that led on deck. The ice-breaking party were working aft—as he had hoped—and the fore-deck was deserted. As he peered into the shadow of the flying bridge he could see the slips that held the bracelets in place, the cast-iron bars delineated sharply in the light of the arc. A couple of blows with the hammer, and the slips would fly out and the bracelets part. Keeping to the shadow of the bridge, he worked his way for'd. It took him less than a minute to reach the bracelets and slips. His hands tightened on the hammer. Only then did the full significance of what he was going to do strike home.

The crew had gone through twenty-four hours of hell to tow the blue as far as they had. What would they think of him if he threw all they had fought for away? For a moment he hesitated. And as he braced himself against the roll of the ship, all the things that he disliked most about whaling came welling up like the creatures of a familiar nightmare out of the storm: the killing of the whales, the harshness of the weather, and, above all, the feeling of not being one of the crew. But then Johan's face, beaded with sweat, came floating by in their wake.

"Hey, there! Keep clear of the slips!"

He sensed the words rather than heard them, but there was no mistaking the gestures of the whaler stumbling toward him.

There was no time to think. He acted by instinct. He stepped back, raised his hammer, and brought it down as

hard as he could on the starboard slip. The iron bar shot into the scuppers. The bracelet parted. And the blue, held now by only a single chain, jerked sideways.

"Hey, deckie!"

He struck again. The second bracelet parted as clean as the first. *Petrel*, freed of the weight of the tow, heeled onto an even keel. And in that moment whale and childhood disappeared forever among the grey Antarctic waves.

He felt neither sorrow nor elation, only a great tiredness such as might be felt by a long-distance runner after a race in which he has pushed body and mind beyond the frontiers of endurance. He was vaguely aware, as a crowd gathered round him, that the tears he had kept for so long in check were streaming unashamed down his face. Then someone took away his hammer, and someone else took him by the hand and led him to the safety of the bridge. Why, they were asking him, had he done it? The tide of questions—some incredulous, some sympathetic, some approving—flooded over him like the maw of a great wave; then suddenly the wave was past, and in silence under the harsh white light of the arc he was face to face with his father.

They stared at one another. Tiredness was building up in John Larsen like water behind a dam. He had done what had had to be done; it was finished, and he now wanted nothing more than to sleep and forget. As his eyes met his father's, he made one final effort to push his tiredness aside. But before he could speak, *Petrel* heeled over in the trough of a wave. He felt himself caught off balance, but he was too tired to care. As the deck plates came rushing up at him he shut his eyes, falling stiff and awkward as a man in an epileptic fit.

His father caught him a fraction of a second before he would have hit the deck.

Svend Larsen thought at first that his son had fainted. Only as he carried him below did he realize he was asleep. They laid him out—for the second time in twenty-four hours—on his bunk, and as they stood round him, uncertain of what to do next, *Petrel* swung head into sea.

Head into sea, pitching rather than rolling, she rode a great deal easier. And when the whalers could see there was no risk of John Larsen tumbling out of his bunk, they left him, splayed out like a starfish as he slept the sleep of the utterly exhausted.

And soon Johan slept too. With his leg still, the bones no longer grating together and the long hours of his agony ended at last, he lay on his back, smiling at the thunder and surge of cattle over the sun-drenched plains of his dreams.

They slept all that day and most of the following night as *Petrel*, head into the waves and free of the tow, rode out the dying hours of the storm in something approaching comfort. By the small hours of Wednesday, April 9, wind and sea had diminished sufficiently for Larsen to head, once again, for the factory ship. But the season by then had ended.

Epilogue
Wednesday, April 9th

John Larsen was woken, as he had been woken every
morning since the season began, by the talk and movement of the whalers who shared his cabin. He opened
his eyes to the soft blue glow of the night lights and
screwed up his nose at the rubbery smell of oilskins.
Nothing, he thought, has changed. They didn't do much
talking as they dressed—4:30 A.M. is not an hour con-
ducive to small talk—but from the few remarks that
were made he gathered that the storm had eased off, that
they were again en route for *Cyclopean*, and that Johan
had slept round the clock. By four forty-five they were
dressed and climbing on deck.

It was bitterly cold; but the clouds had lifted and
broken during the night, the wind had dropped to little
more than a breeze, and the waves had lost their malevolence—even beam into sea, *Petrel* was riding them
smoothly. It was the hour of the false dawn, with every-

thing very still and very quiet, as ice field and sea lane lay waiting for the recurrent miracle of dawn. On *Petrel's* foredeck rime lay thick as a fall of snow, and outside the galley the crew were beginning to queue for their tea.

The boy didn't join them at once but went aft to the saloon where he found that Johan was still asleep—he had been asleep, said the whaler sitting beside him, for fourteen hours; every time he showed signs of waking they doped him with spoonfuls of aspirin soaked in rum. He would have liked to talk to Johan, but he knew very well that it was better to let him sleep, so he clambered back to the foredeck, and when he was sure that the rest of the crew had been given their tea he went to the door of the galley.

"Morning, Torstein!" He held out his mug.

"Morning, John!" The mate took the boy's mug and filled it not quite to the brim with tea; then, very carefully, he tipped in a measure of rum.

It was not in John Larsen's nature to make a parade of his feelings. He simply said "Thank you" and walked across with his drink to where the rest of the crew were sheltering in the lee of the bridge. Here he did exactly as they did: stamping his feet, turning his back to the wind, blowing away the steam, and exchanging traditional jokes with them about the joys of the rising before the sun. And as they laughed and talked together, all of one company, content stole up on him unawares and at the time he was least expecting it.

His tea was bitter, but he drank it all, and when he had

finished it he walked to the rail and watched the sun as it came climbing out of the ice. It rose like a Catherine wheel of the gods, flinging great shafts of gold into a turquoise sky. And as he stared at the sunrise John Larsen became suddenly aware of its beauty, the beauty which had been there each dawn for those who had eyes to see. Why, he asked himself in wonder, had he never seen it before? The sunrise couldn't have changed—that he was sure of; so the change must be in him. He remembered then what Johan had told him: that beauty was in the eye of the beholder.

It was dawn, and all around him in the warmth of the rising sun Antarctica was stirring to life: krill adart through the shallows, penguin astir among the floes, and petrel shearwaters and shoemakers rising and wheeling in ragged echelons above the shore. And in the boy things were stirring, too, as seeds hitherto dormant began to put out root.

He wasn't able that morning to appreciate all that Antarctica had to offer or to understand all the mystique of being one of a crew. But in the gold of the dawn and in his new-found sense of companionship he *was* able to catch a glimpse of why men always came back, year after year, to Antarctica. And it came to him, in a moment of surprise, that it might be possible for him to come back, too, and be happy.

It was not that his dreams had faded or died—his love of music was far too deeply ingrained for that. But he could, now he was a man, look back on those dreams and recognize them for what they had been: the roseate hallucinations of a child. For he had expected something for nothing; he had wanted happiness handed him on a plate, with his father magically paying his fees and with success as a musician coming to him like a birthright. But life, he understood now, simply didn't happen that way; anything worth while had to be fought for, and earned. And it came to him suddenly that if ever in the future he *did* get to the Academy, he would appreciate it all the more. Maybe in time, he thought, I might save up enough to pay for my own tuition, but in the meanwhile at least I can see that the Academy isn't the *only* place in the world where I can learn something worth while.

As the light gained in intensity he watched the crew making good the damage caused by the storm—dislodging ice, greasing the Svend Foyn, straightening the buckled flanges and guardrail. After a while the brothers Carl and Bengt began to unlash the flag markers from the rail and carry them aft for cleaning. The flag markers were heavy.

"John," Bengt Nielsen called, "would you give us a hand?"

He went across to them, and the three whalers lifted the markers and, silhouetted against the gold of the sun, carried them aft together.

As they passed the bridge the boy looked up and saw that his father was watching them, smiling. And happiness—to which he had for so long been a stranger—stole slowly over him. For his father's smile was familiar. It was the same proud, gentle and approving smile that in years long gone by he had seen on the face of his mother.